EVANDER

Immortal Highlander Book 3

HAZEL HUNTER

HH ONLINE

Hazel loves hearing from readers!
You can contact her at the links below.

Website: hazelhunter.com

Facebook:
business.facebook.com/HazelHunterAuthor

Newsletter: HazelHunter.com/news

I send newsletters with details on new releases,
special offers, and other bits of news related to my
writing. You can sign up here!

Chapter One

✌❀✌

RACHEL INGRAM WALKED out
onto the garden balcony overlooking
the swimming pavilion, where her
father's infinity pool spread like a lake suspended
in the air. Beyond it his beloved red gum euca-
lyptus trees climbed the curves of the estate's
rolling green hills. They provided an illusion of
privacy, as if all the world belonged to Avalon.
Sometimes, looking out at the pristine grounds
beneath the porcelain blue sky, it seemed as if
it did.

In Rancho Santa Fe, one of America's wealthiest towns, all of the residents wanted that illusion.
In the Covenant, the most exclusive neighbor-
hood within its boundaries, they got it.

A hundred acres beyond the Ingrams' treasured old trees and high, sculpted hedges lay other immense estate houses belonging to their billionaire neighbors. No one went to the tech mogul's smart mansion to ask for a spare charger, or to the self-help guru's opulent villa to borrow a cup of sugar. That was simply not done. Plenty of neighbors went to the Olympic gold medalist's gaudy shrine to himself and his sport, but he was more of a sociable guy.

"He's holding another party in that over-sized frat house," Sheldon Ingram had often complained to his wife and daughter. "I can hear them rolling the kegs from here."

Rachel smelled the airy sweetness of her mother's white roses, and glanced over hundreds of blooms draping the loggia. Her parents' lounge chairs still sat beside the old stone table that Beatrice Ingram had fallen in love with during their European honeymoon. Her father had secretly shipped it from Scotland to present it to his wife on their first anniversary, along with Avalon.

A few withered petals had fallen on the massive slab of green-streaked granite, which now looked like a toppled tombstone overgrown with moss.

The scent of a familiar, leathery cologne

drifted around her as quiet footsteps approached, and she braced herself against the railing.

"Good morning, Paul."

"I'm so sorry to disturb you, Rachel." Her parents' attorney came to join her, his sober suit fitted as if he'd been born with navy silk as an outer shell. "How are you feeling?"

She wanted to tell him that she'd spent the morning throwing up, but he didn't need to hear that.

"I'm all right, I guess."

"I thought I'd stop in and see if you'd come to a decision about the estate." His smile turned slightly uneasy. "I understand how difficult this must be for you, but the buyer is hoping for an answer on their offer soon."

Difficult? Rachel frowned. Avalon had killed her parents. She had to sell it, only because no one would let her bulldoze it into the ground. But she couldn't say that to Paul Carver. Deliberately destroying a multi-million dollar mansion instead of selling it wasn't acceptable, and in a few hours Paul would be her father-in-law.

No one wanted crazy in the family.

"I can't deal with the sale today," she said. "David and I are going into the city to get married. Then we're going to drive up and spend the weekend at the beach house." She hated how dreary she sounded, talking about her wedding as if it were a dental appointment. Since the funerals she felt so exhausted and depressed, and sometimes just getting out of bed took all her strength. "I'm sorry."

"Keeping it simple is probably best," the attorney said quickly. He agreed with everything she said but, now that she had inherited the Ingram fortune, everyone except David was doing that. "Call me when you get back in town, and then we'll talk." He touched her shoulder before he retreated inside the mansion.

A few minutes later the purring sound of a Rolls came from the front of the house, and Rachel watched as the man who would be her father-in-law sped down the long curving drive, pausing only for security to open the gates.

For once Paul's behavior actually registered as odd to her. It seemed as if he couldn't get away from her and Avalon fast enough, and she wondered why. Her father had made Paul a very wealthy man, and Rachel was marrying his son. Maybe he didn't want her to, or he simply didn't like her. Yet when she'd told him they were getting married, she'd felt his relief as surely as if he'd voiced it.

Rachel had often wondered if she should tell her fiancé about her uncanny intuition. But David might think she was delusional, and over the last few weeks her sensitivity had been so muted she rarely even felt her own emotions. His father had to be happy about the marriage. If nothing else, Rachel was now one of the richest women in the country.

It was all thanks to her dad, who had used the millions he inherited from his corporate CEO father to become the most successful start-up investor in modern history. From solar-powered smart phones to 3-D printed replacement heart valves, the ventures Sheldon Ingram bankrolled always proved wildly innovative as well as profitable in the extreme.

"I'm not a genius," Sheldon told a reporter once. "I invest in people. Guessing which ones are going to change the world is what I do best."

Her father had slowed down only long enough to romance and marry Beatrice, Rachel's Italian heiress mother, who had brought old world money, blue blood, and ancient connections with European royalty as her dowry. He'd built this

Mediterranean chateau for her when she'd gotten pregnant with Rachel, called it Avalon, and then set up his kingdom in the Covenant.

Her father had always fancied himself a Merlin rather than a King Arthur. Since everything he touched turned to gold, Midas might have been more appropriate. Thanks to him, Rachel would never have to work, or worry, or do anything except what she wanted.

But all she wanted was what she could never again have.

Rachel would happily give every cent she'd inherited to hear once more the reassurance of her father's deep voice, and the sweet trill of her mother's easy laughter. They had given her so much love she'd never once considered how it would feel to be without it. She would beggar herself to bring them back to life. If only she'd skipped the weekend shopping trip to L.A. with David and his mother. She'd have been here when the fire started. She knew she would have woken up in time to get them out of the house—or not.

I could have died with them.

How long Rachel stood there wishing for what she could never have, she didn't know. She only came out of her trance when her fingers began to cramp, and glanced down to see the white-knuckled grip she had on the balcony railing. Carefully she released it and turned around to face Avalon, now fully cleaned and restored. The only signs of the electrical fire that had consumed the master suite and burned her parents to death was scorched earth around the newly-built wing. In another week the landscaping company would finish putting in the new sod, and even that would be gone.

Like her parents, cremated in their own bed.

"Darling?"

From inside the sunroom David Carver emerged, his elegant hands holding two slender goblets of champagne. From his razor-cut short blond hair to his spotless white shirt and shorts he looked immaculate, but then he always did. Rachel knew he had spent the morning playing tennis at one of his mother's charity fundraisers, and yet he still appeared pressed and polished, as if he'd just gotten dressed.

Rachel admired his perfection—who didn't? —but something about his appearance this morning bothered her. He seemed almost too spotless. Did her fiancé even have the ability to sweat?

"Are we toasting your victory?" she asked.

One thing that had attracted her to David was that, like a very few other people, she could never read him. For her that felt intriguing, as well as very restful.

"No, I lost my only match to that actor from Star Wars," David said, rolling his pale brown eyes as he came to hand her one of the flutes. "I stayed to watch Mother beat the club pro in straight sets." His smile sparkled. "Revenge for him criticizing her backhand, I think."

Guilt knotted Rachel's stomach. Marianne Carver had been so kind to her since the fire, and she hadn't even considered going to the fundraiser.

"Your dad was here earlier. I think we should have invited your parents to come to the ceremony today."

Why hadn't she even thought about that before now?

"Rache, darling, they understand." His gaze shifted to the rebuilt wing, and he curled an arm around her shoulders. "This is just a formality. Once you've had time to grieve, and you're ready to do the big, beautiful wedding you deserve, then

we'll have our family and friends there to celebrate with us."

David meant to be reassuring, but it only
brought home to her that since leaving college
she'd lost touch with all of her old friends. She
liked the Carvers well enough, but it was hard to
think of Paul or Marianne as her in-laws or
parents. They didn't seem like parents at all.
Maybe once she and David were married for a
while her feelings would change, but for now she
felt completely alone. It wasn't self-pity, either.
Her parents had been the last living members of
both their families. Rachel had no relatives left.

Still, she knew getting married now was the
right thing to do. She had so many decisions to
make about her massive inheritance, and the
constant daze she'd been in since the funeral had
only made those pile up. She also wanted to make
her own mark on the world, the way her father
had, by making her family's money work to help
people. David agreed. He'd told her more than
once that the best thing they could do was carry on
her father's legacy and make dreams come true.

"To our future," he said now, holding out his
glass. "And our wedding day."

Rachel touched her rim to his. Their marriage had been the only thing she'd had to look forward to, and she desperately wanted to be happy again. David had stayed at her side through the darkest days of her life, so she already knew he would be a good husband. She might not be able to read him, but everything he did told her how much he loved her and wanted to take care of her. The only thing that worried her was something they hadn't yet done.

They'd never made love.

It seemed ridiculously old-fashioned, but David had persuaded her to save their first time together until after they were married. What he claimed would be deeply romantic had always made Rachel feel a little nervous. With just two boyfriends under her belt she didn't have a lot of experience with men, but she'd liked sex. Her attraction to David hadn't been physical, exactly, but she'd been looking forward to being intimate with him. She'd even secretly practiced a few things.

What would she do if they turned out to be a disaster in bed?

"You're not drinking to us," David said, and

took a sip from his glass as he watched her face. "Second thoughts?"

"It feels like I just buried my parents, and you and I have never… It's all happening so fast," she finished, feeling awkward now. "I know I've been a mess, really I do. God, I can't even remember when you proposed to me."

"Hey." He gave her arm a soothing caress. "I'm not going to push you into anything, Rache. But please, at least drink to our future—unless you're planning to jilt me at the Justice of the Peace."

She took a swallow, grimacing at the acrid taste of the champagne.

"I'm not, I promise."

"Poor darling," he cooed and pressed a gentle kiss on her brow. "Tell you what, let's forget about the wedding and head up to the beach house. We can spend the weekend sunning ourselves and making love."

She stared into his eyes, which the sunlight had turned to gold. His sudden change of heart made her feel dizzy. Or maybe it was drinking on an empty stomach.

"You told me that you wanted to wait until our wedding night."

"I did, didn't I? Come here." David folded his arms around her and rested his cheek on the top of her head. "Honestly, darling, I don't think I can keep my hands off you another day."

Rachel felt so relieved she nearly wept. He smelled crisp and clean, and she just wanted to wrap him around her and breathe him in. But she also wanted the wedding behind her.

"I'm sorry," she finally said. "I think I must be suffering from a case of the jitters."

"You're allowed, my beautiful bride." He held her for a few minutes before he set her at arm's length, and smiled. "Now what will it be: a long sexy weekend on the beach as new lovers, or newly-weds?"

As she looked at him, she had another of her intuitions. He really was her future, and it was high time she got to it.

"Marry me," she said.

Chapter Two

✿❧✿

G ETTING MARRIED AT the county
administration center in downtown
San Diego took only an hour. Rachel
wore a simple cream-colored skirt and blazer over
an ivory silk chemise. Although it was Chanel, it
felt almost too plain for a wedding, but she didn't
have anything else in her wardrobe that was
white. To her relief the ceremony proved to be
very short and unsentimental, barely more than
the exchange of their simple gold bands. By the
time the clerk handed David their marriage
license Rachel felt exhausted. She hoped she
could get in a nap on the drive to the beach
house.

"Would you like a commemorative photograph, sir?" the middle-aged secretary who stood as their witness asked. "It's ten dollars."

David chuckled and shook his head. "You people already tapped me for eighty bucks. I have to save the rest of my cash to spend on my new wife. Now where is your notary public?"

"Room four-oh-two on the fourth floor," the secretary said.

On the way up in the elevator Rachel watched her new husband take an envelope from his jacket. Had he mentioned the notary before?

"What do you need to have notarized?"

"I need to grant you power of attorney," David said, and sighed. "It's gruesome, I know, but my father says with all the traveling I do it's important to have one in place. If something happens to me, you'll be able to access my accounts, sell my stocks, and that sort of thing. Naturally my wealth can't compare to your father's, but I'm about to have a big investment pay off, so it'll give me some peace of mind."

That he trusted her this much deeply touched her. "David, I don't know what to say."

He shrugged. "It's what you do when you get married."

In the notary's office Rachel reached into her

purse for her reading glasses, only to discover she'd left them back at the house.

"Oh, I forgot my glasses."

"I can read it to you, if you want," David offered.

Her stomach churned as a wave of dizziness came over her. If she didn't get out of here soon, she was going to vomit all over the notary's desk.

"No, that's all right. Just show me where I sign."

After pointing to the signature line for her, David asked the clerk, "Could you make an extra copy of this for us, so my wife can read it later?"

By the time they left the building and got to the car Rachel felt as if she might keel over. She dropped into her seat with a grateful groan.

"I don't know why I feel like this," she told David as he climbed in behind the wheel. She swiped at the sweat on her brow and grimaced. "Maybe I should see a doctor."

"Take a nap while I drive," he suggested. "If you still feel sick when we get to Monterey, we'll call your family doctor, and have him come out to the house."

Rachel hated making a fuss, so she nodded. "All right. Thanks for understanding."

He started the engine and grinned at her. "Thank you, my darling, for not jilting me. You just made me one of the richest men in the world."

She forced a laugh, but he sounded almost as if he were gloating.

"So the truth finally comes out," she said. "You married me for my money."

"I married *you*," he corrected her, wagging a finger, "not your inheritance." She noticed the sunlight glinting from his wedding band. "If you like, when we get back you can donate your billions to the homeless. We'll live off my income, which should keep you in Chanel, as long as you shop at the outlets."

His obvious amusement made her feel a little better. "Okay."

Rachel settled back in her seat and watched as he drove through the city to the interstate. When he switched on some of the classic music he liked, she closed her eyes. Nightmares about Avalon burning had turned her into an insomniac, but now she felt as if the horror was at last coming to an end. A moment later she drifted off into a deep, dreamless sleep.

Sometime later the feel of the car stopping

woke her. She felt a little confused when she looked out and saw the setting sun streaming through a grove of massive oaks.

"This isn't Monterey," she said smothering a yawn.

"We're in Los Padres," David told her as he unclipped her seat belt before he climbed out of the car and came around to open her door.

Rachel shouldered her purse and got out, but was shocked by how unsteady her legs felt.

"Oh, I still don't feel very well."

"Take my arm," David said and guided her into the grove. "That's it. You just need some food and fresh air, which is why we're having a picnic."

She frowned as she spotted the red and white checked cloth on the ground, and the big picnic hamper beside it.

"Who set this up?"

"That would be me," David admitted. "I lied about going to the club this morning. I came here instead to arrange everything. I had to do this, Rache. After all, this is the best day of my life."

Vague memories of chasing butterflies through a meadow came back to Rachel. As she and David moved through the dappled light cascading down through the old oaks she saw one crooked limb forming an arch, and finally recognized the place.

"This was my parents' favorite picnic spot when I was a little girl," she said, turning toward her husband. "How did you know about it?"

"Your father told me," David said, and tugged her to a stop just before they reached the picnic basket. "He wanted me to bring you here when I was ready to propose, but I decided to save it for a bigger surprise. Now close your eyes, and don't move."

A sudden, inexplicable apprehension shivered through her, but Rachel ignored it and dutifully obeyed him.

"Should I guess what the surprise is?"

"You'll never be able to do that," he assured her, his voice moving away from her.

Rachel's head felt a little clearer now, and some of what he'd told her wasn't making much sense. Her father hadn't been especially fond of David, and more than once before he'd died had advised her not to rush into anything with him. So why would he suggest David propose to her at all, much less at such a private family spot? And why was her skin now crawling with goosebumps?

"When did you and my dad talk about this?" she asked.

"It was the day I asked for his permission to marry you." David's footsteps shuffled through the grass as he returned to stand behind her. "He didn't say yes, if you're wondering. He never liked me very much. I have to admit, that always rankled a bit. Parents usually love me."

"He was just being an over-protective father, I guess." She swayed a little on her feet. "So what's the big surprise?"

"Something you never once suspected, I'm happy to say." His hand ran from her nape to a spot between her shoulder blades, and stopped to press against a space in her spine. "Okay, here it is."

Rachel's eyes flew open as something long and sharp rammed into her back and skewered her. She screamed as everything below her ribs went completely dead. David gave her a hard shove onto the checked cloth, which fell with her into the ground, and then yanked the cloth out from under her, turning her face-up in the shallow pit.

"David, I can't move." Rachel felt as if she had shrieked the words, but they sounded slurred and choked. She couldn't understand why he just stood there watching her. "Please, help me."

"You can't move because your spinal cord is severed." Her husband neatly folded the table-cloth as he looked down at her, his expression serene. "You still don't get it, do you? God, you're a complete dupe. I stabbed you in the back, Rachel. I'm *murdering* you." He chuckled, shook his head, and moved out of her sight.

As her chest hitched Rachel stared up at the black, twisted branches of the grove's canopy. He'd come here this morning. He'd planned this. Everything he'd said and done had been to bring her here and do this. The man she loved had never loved her. This was the reason she'd never been able to pick up on his emotions. He didn't have any that were real.

She'd married a psychopath.

The sound of a trunk slamming shut made her peer at the edge of the pit. David appeared a minute later holding a large shovel.

"You really had me sweating when you tried to back out this morning, you know," he said, smiling. "I'm glad I talked you out of that. Now, I'm not sure if you'll smother before you bleed out, but either way, I don't care. I only need you dead."

She didn't have to ask him why. Of course it was her money. A knot of agony tightened inside her lungs. It was hard to breathe, and her numb body chilled as if she were already dead. Clots of dirt landed on top of her as he began filling in the pit. Rachel dragged in as much air as she could.

"How could you…do this?"

"Jesus, how could I not?" he countered cheerfully. "My gambling debts have grown rather mountainous, and the showgirl I've been screwing in Vegas got pregnant and is suing me for child support. My father threatened to disown me if I didn't find a rich wife to bail me out. Did you know he told me all about you, the sweet, shy heiress to billions? Babe, you were practically begging to make me an insanely wealthy widower."

"They'll know…you did it," she told him, and choked as the next shovelful landed on her face. "Paul…will tell."

"Dad won't say a word, and they're never going to find your body, you idiotic twat."

He stopped shoveling and knelt down to remove her shoes, and then wrenched off her wedding ring. She couldn't feel his touch, for which she was grateful.

"Why…not?"

"I thought about using fire again, but they'll never look for you here. Tonight I'll make it look like you drowned while you were swimming at the beach house, and the currents swept away your body." He stood up. "I am sorry that I never fucked you, but as rough as I am in bed, I couldn't risk it. Even with the drugs I've been giving you, you probably would have dumped me afterward."

He sounded so smug but her shock and horror dwindled as she realized his mistake. He'd removed her ring but not the–

The pain deep inside her chest swelled, growing as hot as an open flame, and her heartbeat fluttered like a moth dashing itself against it.

"Smart," she wheezed. The whistling sounds coming from deep in her chest. When they ended, so would she. "Hope it's…worth it."

"Please, just shut up and die," David said, working faster with the shovel.

The soil he mounded over her soon filled her eyes and nose and mouth, and Rachel stopped fighting it. Her lungs flattened, and her pulse slowed, and the iciness of her paralyzed body made her feel as if she had turned to stone. Inside her head she could see the oak grove, which seemed to be swirling into the shape of a tunnel.

Yearning flickered through her confused thoughts. Would she see her parents again? She didn't care about David or what he had done anymore. She was ready to go to the next place. She didn't know if it would be like heaven, or a new life, but she hoped it would be better than this. Anything would be.

A glowing light filled the whirling tunnel of leaves and arching branches, outlining the form of a tall man standing between two moons: one white, and the other black. The lethal-looking spear he held in his strong hand bent into the shape of a letter Z turned on its side. Over it his dark green eyes met hers, and somehow Rachel knew what he was thinking.

'Tis time. I've naught left to me, lass. I cannae go on pretending I do.

Images of a dark-haired woman poured into Rachel's mind. Her body appeared first voluptuous, and then slowly grew thinner. Her pretty face tightened into a gaunt, worried mask, and then went ashen. The last image of her was in a bed surrounded by candles. Her lips were blistered and her face covered with open sores, her chest barely rising and falling before it went still.

The man came to kneel beside the bed, and buried his face in the dead woman's sweat-dampened hair. A flood of despair and love poured into Rachel, and she finally understood. He had loved the woman, and he didn't want to live without her.

No. She stretched out her hand to him. *Wait. Don't do it.*

The dark-haired woman floated past her, and then the ground rose up and swallowed Rachel alive.

Chapter Three

O AK LEAVES RUSTLED in the cold wind as Evander Talorc made his way across the sacred grove. The moon had risen full and bright in the sky, silvering everything with its cool light, but he no longer cared if anyone saw him. As he approached the spot where he had buried the woman he had loved, nothing much concerned him.

He'd made his choice. This night his torment would end.

The ancient stones stood as if guarding the unmarked grave of Fiona Marphee. The Pritani designs carved on their weathered surfaces caught the moonlight and edged it with shadow. Like him, they had come into the world hard and cold, wrenched from the womb of the mother to be hewn and etched by powerful forces. He'd often thought if he'd stood still long enough he'd become one of them. That they would watch over his lady from this night on gave him a little solace.

"Fair evening, love," Evander said as he bent to place the bouquet of white heather in the cool grass, and then straightened to watch the tiny petals shiver in the wind. "'Tis been weeks, I ken, but the roof wanted mending. That little owl has taken to the barn rafters again. I expect he'll winter there. I left your gray with the man who bought the sheep farm. He'll look after her. You were right about the gorse. They've crept up through your heather now."

He'd bloodied his hands, trying to weed all of the prickly yellow blooms out of the flower beds she'd planted. He knew by the next moon the frost would come to take it all, but he couldn't bear seeing the life choked out of her heather. Not when he'd watched his love do the same to Fiona.

Evander had risked everything to be with his mortal lover, turning his back on his duty and his clan to run away with her. They'd gone as far from the Isle of Skye as they could, first hiding in the lowlands near Aberbrothock before traveling to the eastern highlands near Wick. He'd scoured the lochs and rivers until he'd gathered enough gold nuggets to buy an old shepherd's cottage in the mountains, a few miles above a small seaside village. The local mortals, most of whom were descended from Viking raiders, tolerated their infrequent visits to buy necessary goods. Evander in turn remained civil but watchful.

They'd taken the name Hunter, but in truth they were the hunted.

Despite his efforts to make Fiona feel safe, she had fretted and worried every day about their future. Since their escape she had been convinced that they would be pursued, captured, and executed for what they had done. Every noise made her flinch. Every visitor sent her into a panic. Yet in the end their enemies never found them.

Death did.

There had been no warning that sickness had struck the old shepherd's farm. Fiona only went there every few months to buy wool for her weaving, which she made into the blankets and coverlets that Evander took into town to sell. He always went with her, but for some reason on her final trip she'd waited until he went hunting before going alone. He'd heard her screaming, and rushed back to the cottage to find her filthy and hysterical.

"They're all dead, even the bairns," she'd sobbed against his chest. "I tripped and fell on the shepherd's wife. The pox had eaten away her face–" She tore at the front of her gown. "Take this off me. She's all over it."

Evander had stripped her and scrubbed her clean, and for more than a week after that Fiona seemed well. His hope ended when he woke one morning to find her thrashing beside him, and saw the tell-tale dimpled lesions covering her arms and face. He'd wiped down her hot body and coaxed her into swallowing some broth, and lay with her until she came to her senses.

"I'm done for now, lad," she said, her lovely eyes clouded by fever.

"'Tis no' always so bad," Evander said. But he knew if she survived she would be badly disfig-ured. It didn't matter to him. She had become his whole world, and without her he would have nothing left. He would *be* nothing. "You're young and strong, sweetheart, and I'll look after you."

"You still dinnae ken," she muttered, and then rested one thin hand against his cheek. "The gods are taking me, and freeing you. 'Tis how it should end, Evander."

"Now you're talking daft," he said and brushed the hair back from her pocked brow. "You'll survive this. You've been through worse."

"When I'm gone, put me in the grove," Fiona said and closed her eyes. "The gods will forgive what I've done if you give me to the oaks. I want to sleep with them."

"No," he said and pressed her hand to his mouth. "Stay with me. Let my love be your strength."

She shook her head. "You were ever my weakness."

In the end his love and care had done nothing for her. The plague had ravaged her body before it had filled her lungs and choked the breath from her three days later. He'd left her for a moment to fetch water, and when he returned she'd gone. At times he wondered if she'd waited for him to leave so she could die without him watching it.

It had been almost six months now, and grief no longer stabbed him in the heart when he paid a visit to her grave. In the beginning he came every week to sit with her, and talk of how well her garden was growing, and the improvements he had made to their little cottage. Sometimes he stretched out beside her and simply looked up at the stars. But each time he returned to the grove he felt his heart grow heavier. Fiona could not hear him, and she was never coming back. When he spoke, it was only his ears that heard him. The days and nights he spent at the cottage had begun to blur together, while the world around him seemed to be graying and flattening. Everything he forced himself to eat tasted the same. He'd even tried getting drunk, but after half a jug of whiskey he'd only felt numb.

Evander could no longer bear his loneliness.

It should stop now, this miserable immortal existence of his. The finality of it made a darkness swell in his heart. He had been angry and foolish, and he had betrayed the men who had given him a home and purpose. Fiona was gone, and the gods would never offer him another chance of happiness. Whatever rewards awaited in the after-life, none had been saved for him. He fully expected to be damned to oblivion.

"'Tis time," he murmured. "I've naught left to me, lass. I cannae go on pretending I do. I mean to hunt the undead, and kill as many as I may before they take me." Dying that way, in battle, was the only honorable way to end his life. It would also give him the chance to do a little good before he went. "I am no' sorry I loved you. You made me a better man, Fiona. Be at rest now, lass."

Beneath his tunic the ink of his war spirit woke, but for the first time since he had been inked it did not fill him with anger and blood lust. Instead it pulled at him, as if it meant to drag him to the ground. He glanced down.

Dirt fell away from a slender hand pushing up out of the ground, the fingers clawing at the air.

"*Fiona.*"

Evander fell to his knees, gouging at the soil around the hand until he exposed an arm, and then a shoulder, and uncovered a face. Frantically he wiped the dirt away, stilling as he realized the features were not Fiona's. This woman had an angular face and a squared jaw, and her brows arched over large, thickly-lashed eyes.

A howl of rage rose in his throat, that the gods would be so cruel to give him such hope, and then such crushing desolation.

"Please," she gasped.

Eyes so dark they looked like black pearls opened and stared up at him, reflecting everything he felt. Earth soiled every inch of her, and she smelled of rot. Yet when her blackened hand clutched at his, it tore at his heart. Someone had done this sickening thing to her, and it had not been the gods.

"I have you," he said.

He worked his arms under her, and dragged her up, freeing her from her grave. He did what he could to brush away the soil from her strange white garments. Her skirt must have been hacked off her, exposing legs clad in hose so thin it looked to be spun from spider web. She wore no shoes, but she smelled of roses and earth now.

As he placed her on her feet she turned, revealing the back of her clothes had been soaked with fresh blood—so much that he could hardly believe she yet lived.

"Be still," he said. "You are injured."

"I'm not," she said but looked down at her legs and then at Evander. "I can move. I'm not dead." Her brows drew together. "I should be dead."

Evander scowled, for her oddly-accented voice

sounded exactly like Kinley Chandler, the female soldier from the future. Two years past Kinley had come through this very time portal to save the life of his laird, Lachlan McDonnel. And tonight Evander had come here to bid his lover farewell before he sought his own end. He looked down into the grave that he had dug for Fiona, but it remained empty. Only the shield he had placed under his lover's head remained.

Evander gripped her arms. "Were you sent? Do the gods mean to torment me? Why do you come here?" When her eyes widened he shook her. *"Tell me."*

Her eyes rolled back into her head and she dropped.

Evander kept her from collapsing, holding her against him as he fell to his knees and swore over her drooping head. The warmth of her bloody clothes made it clear she had been hurt only moments before in her time, yet when he carefully felt along her back he found no wounds. She had a tear in the back of her short white coat that seemed to be the source of the blood, but his fingers found only soft, unbroken skin beneath it. To be sure he dragged up the coat and the thin garment beneath it, exposing the long line of her spine. He couldn't find a mark on her.

What had healed her? Evander glanced up at the ancient oaks, and felt his blood chill. Fiona had told him stories about the magic of the groves, tales he'd dismissed as superstitions. Could this place have healed the woman? Or had it been the gods themselves?

As Evander checked for her heartbeat, he felt the skin across his chest vibrating. Beneath his tunic his war spirit pulsed, hungry for violence and vengeance.

A low sound came from the woman, and her black lashes fluttered as she came out of the faint. She went stiff against him, and fear made her mouth tight, but she did not struggle.

"I shouldnae have shouted," he said, his voice flinty. "You've done naught wrong." It had been so long since he'd spoken to another person that he hardly knew what to say. "Tell me your name."

"Rachel Ingram," she said and glanced around them. "Where am I?"

Evander wanted to curse the gods for bringing the woman to him, if they had indeed sent her.

"You've come to the Scottish highlands, Mistress Ingram." He waited for her to react, and when she didn't he wondered if he should tell her the rest. "Did you no' mean to?"

Rachel turned her head toward the hills, and her mouth tightened. "Someone's coming."

Evander looked over and in the distance saw an undead patrol riding in their direction. They must have picked up the scent of Rachel's blood on the wind. His desire to battle them until he was killed swelled, and then just as abruptly dwindled. The smell of the blood would send the undead into a frenzy. They would tear him apart to get at her. His life mattered not, but she was a mortal, and entirely defenseless.

"We should get out of here," she whispered.

"Aye." He lifted her into his arms, and ran with her into the trees to where he'd tethered his red roan stallion. He seated her backward on the front of his saddle before he swung up and gathered the reins. He could see her confusion. "You must hold onto me and no' let go, even for an instant. Can you do that?"

Rachel nodded and wrapped her arms around him, plastering herself against his chest.

The feel of her body against him soothed the savage rage his spirit had spilled into his veins, perplexing Evander. Nothing but burying a spear in the heart of the enemy had ever calmed him when his spirit was aroused, but there was no time to fathom it now. He touched his heels to his mount's sides, and guided the horse through the forest to the bank of the stream.

"Close your eyes," he told her, "and hold your breath."

Since leaving the clan Evander had trained the roan in the old way, to accompany him when he used his ability to bond with water and travel through it. Before they had grown wealthy enough to keep horses on the mainland, the clan had always trained and taken their mounts into the waters with them. As he no longer had access to the clan's mainland stables Evander had no choice but to take his mounts with him. He felt Rachel jerk as he changed and took her and the horse beneath the surface with him, where he pulled them through the currents as he thought of the small loch near his cottage in the north. A moment later they rode out of the churning, bubbling waves and onto the bank. Rachel didn't move, and when he tilted up her chin he saw she still had her eyes squeezed tightly shut.

"You can look now," he said.

Evander guided the roan up to the cottage's

garden, where he lowered Rachel to the ground before he dismounted. She stood waiting, her hair plastered to her head and her garments dripping wet. The journey through the water had washed the soil from her skin, which appeared flawless. Most of the blood had also been soaked from her clothing, but he could not permit any mortal to see her dressed so. She would be branded a witch.

"Come inside," he said as he opened the gate.

She walked along the slate stones he'd used to make a path through the garden, and when he unlatched the door she entered the dark cottage. He quickly lit a fire in the hearth, and led her over to it before he retrieved his robe.

"Take off your clothes," he told her without thinking, and then added. "So you dinnae become chilled and sick." He held out the robe. "Put this on after you do."

He hated the terse, grating sound of his voice in the stillness. Why was she so silent? Had he frightened her so much?

Rachel silently stripped out of her outer garments, beneath which she wore tiny trews and some manner of breast-shaped band. When Evander realized he was staring, he averted his gaze. Once she had wrapped his robe around herself she swayed on her feet, as if she meant to faint again. He took her arm and guided her to his big chair.

"Sit and rest," he said.

Once she did, he gathered her garments and squeezed the water from them before he pitched them into the flames. He glanced at her, expecting an angry protest, but she simply watched him with her big, dark eyes. Her stillness unnerved him, until he recalled that Rachel likely had no understanding of where she was or what had happened to her.

"My name is Evander Talorc, and I will tell what I ken." He drew over a stool and sat before her. "The grove where I found you is a portal through the ages, and brought you here from your time to mine. We're in the Scottish highlands, and you've come to the year thirteen sixteen." He waited a moment for her to react, and when she didn't he said, "You are not the first to journey here from the future. That you could cross over means that you are druid kind, for only they may use the groves for such journeys. Do you ken of the magic folk?"

Rachel said nothing, but curled her hands into fists.

Evander silently cursed himself for saying too much. "I'll no' harm you, Mistress. My clan, my people, protect yours. 'Twill all be well." He rose and retrieved a bottle of wine, a goblet and a loaf of bread from the pantry, and brought both to her. "Here." Yet when he poured the wine for her, and broke off a piece of the bread, she didn't move to take either from him. "'Tis no' to your liking? Do you want water? Fruit? There are apples and pears, I reckon."

She stared past him into the flames as if she no longer heard him, her bottom lip caught in the edge of her teeth.

What had she said in the grove? *I can move. I'm not dead. I should be dead.*

Evander drew back, and suddenly all of the oddities about her came together to paint a dire portrait. Perhaps she had been injured and alive when she had been put in the ground, and her druid blood activated the time portal. Thus she had been transported here, still trapped in the earth. The horror she must have felt to awake thus was what had made her so compliant. Rachel wasn't afraid of him. She no longer heard him. Her own terror held her fast in its grip. He reached out to touch her, and then thought better of it.

"You've been made whole and well, Mistress Ingram. I cannae tell you how, and it doesnae seem so to you now, but the gods have smiled upon you." And cursed him with her care, it seemed.

When she said nothing he went to fill the goblet with water from the kitchen urn. He should take her down to the village, and have them summon a druid from the nearest settlement. The magic folk would know what to do with her. Yet he had told her his name, and she might repeat it.

Evander saw the water overflowing from the goblet to the counter and slammed down the urn. He'd never had any patience with wenches, nor had he the belly for nursing one who had gone daft. Still, the wee lass had been trapped in the earth. That would make mad even the strongest of men.

As soon as he returned to Rachel, he smelled fresh blood, and saw drops of it on the planks just before her. On closer inspection he saw that she had knotted her hands so tightly her fingernails had cut into her palms.

"Show me your hands."

When she didn't, he gently pried open her fingers and used the water to wash away the blood, turning her palms toward the firelight to see how deep the gouges were. He felt something warm and wet drop onto the back of his own hand, and looked up to see the tears spilling from her brimming eyes. He had no words to comfort her, and yet still he tried.

"What was done to you is healed, lass. No one shall touch you again. I swear it."

Rachel's lips pressed together, and then she began weeping, her slight frame shaking with the force of her sobs.

Evander lifted her from the chair and sat down to hold her on his lap. He knew nothing of her, so it should have seemed strange to be so familiar. Instead her warmth and slight weight fit against him as if she had been formed for just such an embrace, and made an answering heat rise in his chest. He tucked her head under his chin and rubbed her shoulder and arm with his hand, wishing he knew what more to do to ease her anguish.

His touch alone seemed to soothe Rachel, for she soon calmed and only shuddered now and then as she lay against him. To see her face he had to brush her damp, tangled hair back, and the desolation he saw in her expression wrenched at him.

"You have my word. I'll keep you safe."

"I know you will," she whispered, and touched his hand. "Thank you for saving my life."

He would have to explain to her that her healing had been none of his doing, but her eyes closed, and he heard her breathing slow and felt her body relax. She had fallen asleep in his arms with absolute trust, as if she had always done so. He knew he should carry her into his bed, but after so many months of solitude, holding her and watching her gave him genuine pleasure.

Evander wondered why anyone would harm such a woman, for she must have been a cherished beauty in her time. The firelight shimmered over her, picking out glints of blue and violet in her black tresses, which had dried now. Once combed he imagined it would look like polished jet. He liked the regal straight line of her nose, and the wide, generous curves of her lips. She had chiseled cheekbones that balanced her strong jaw, and skin as luscious as the flesh of a golden pear.

Rachel shifted against him in her sleep, and

his robe fell open to reveal her small, perfect body.

He reached to cover her again, but could not help looking upon her for a long moment before he did. As with her back, he saw no sign of injury. She had slight breasts and slim hips, but her flat belly bore none of the marks from childbirth. The fragile curves of her delicate figure made him think of fine porcelain brought by ships from the east, so rare and exquisite that only the wealthiest of nobles could afford them. Yet even as he admired her elegance, seeing her thus made his blood pulse hot and thick.

Evander had not felt nor thought of his own desires since Fiona had died. Feeling his cock swell for Rachel filled him with such self-loathing that he nearly swore aloud.

She is shocked and frightened and needs care. What you want matters naught. Protect her.

He gathered her against him and stood, carrying her into the bed chamber he had shared with Fiona. After the pox had taken his lover he had burned the linens and mattress, which reminded him too much of her wretched death. For his own comfort he'd made a new mattress with clean straw padded with soft fleece, and bought new linens from the village. Carefully he placed Rachel on the bed, covering her with his old tartan before he stood brooding over her.

She looked so frail and helpless that he wanted nothing more than to lay with her and hold her through the night. That he wanted to do more than that made his gut knot. What manner of man was he, to desire a woman who had been savaged and buried alive and hurled through time?

Get away from her.

Evander needed to retrieve Fiona's gray from the farmer keeping her for him, and then he could sleep in the barn. He also knew he couldn't do either unless he knew Rachel was safe.

"I am sorry for this, lass." He picked up the wedge stones he used to block the narrow window when it snowed, and then went out to close the door to the bed chamber. Bracing Fiona's heavy standing loom against it assured that Rachel would not be able to open it. "'Twill be only for the night."

COZY WARMTH SURROUNDED Rachel as she

opened her eyes to see an odd-looking ceiling above her. It seemed to be some kind of densely-woven thatching made of thin, long branches and bunched grasses. A small spider web occupied one corner, and gleamed like fine silver lace in a bright, narrow beam of sunlight. It felt like morning, but the air around her seemed very cold, and she could smell wood burning.

The bed she lay in looked exactly like the one from her vision of the green-eyed man and the dying woman. She touched an edge of the clean, finely-woven sheet, surprised to find that it had the feel of expensive organic linen. She brought it to her nose and smelled lavender and sunshine, and suddenly her head filled with flashes of memory.

Please, just shut up and die.

Bile burned in Rachel's throat. She could still taste the dirt David had shoveled onto her, and feel the warmth of her own blood spreading across her back. She couldn't have survived what he'd done to her. Frantically she looked around the room. Why was she here? After what her husband had done to her, she should be dead. Was she dead now?

A deep, hard voice cut through those awful thoughts.

I have you.

The warrior she'd seen in her mind had told her his name last night—Evander Talorc. He'd been angry with her for not being Fiona. Still, he'd brought her to safety, and claimed that she'd come to the highlands of Scotland in the fourteenth century. It all seemed so bizarre. Yet he'd told her what he considered the truth. Nothing Evander thought contradicted a word that he'd said to her.

Nothing he thought? How could she know what he'd been thinking?

Rachel pushed herself up in a sitting position, expecting to feel the usual nausea. Her head didn't spin, and her belly remained calm.

Of course I feel well. David isn't around to drug me anymore.

To keep from thinking about him and all the horrible things he'd done to her, which *would* make her puke, she inspected her surroundings. The room she occupied had rough, stained plaster walls, a floor covered by several woven mats, and a few pieces of old, crude furniture. The only window, which appeared to be nothing more than

a long, narrow slit in the thick wall, had been
filled with two heavy-looking, wedge-shaped
rocks. The thick mattress beneath her made
rustling noises when she moved, and smelled of
hay. Atop the linen sheet lay a faded plaid wool
blanket with black and gold stripes on a plum
background.

Everything quietly shrieked fourteenth
century Scotland, too.

"Hello?" When no one answered her Rachel
listened for a moment, but heard nothing. "Is
anyone there?"

A low, masculine voice came to her, but it
wasn't anything she could hear. Instead he spoke
inside her head, as if someone had tucked a tiny
speaker behind her eyes.

*I must be gentle. She will ken naught of this time, and
may fight me as Kinley did the laird when first she came. I
cannae take her back to the grove. If she returns, the
cowardly fack who harmed her may try again. Should I
take her to the magic folk, and ask them to have Cailean
care for her, or send her to Dun Aran, and the clan? Aber
will kill me the moment he sees me. What if she was sent
for me? Why was she in the grove where I buried Fiona?*

With the voice came images of boots pacing
and kicking straw. One horse watched her warily

from its stall, the large reddish-white roan she vaguely recalled from last night. Another smaller, dappled gray with a silky black mane stood waiting to be unsaddled. She caught glimpses of sacks of grain, tack hung neatly from hooks and hand brushes for currying, but all of it looked rough and crude. It also shifted oddly, until she realized she was seeing the barn through someone else's eyes.

Evander's eyes.

Rachel knew she was inside his head, hearing his thoughts, and seeing what he saw. It couldn't be her imagination, not with all the unfamiliar words and names streaming into her mind. She closed her eyes to concentrate, and dredged through her hazy memories to recall everything he'd told her.

None of it made sense. Her blood had allowed her to travel through time? She'd somehow jumped from twenty-first century California to fourteenth-century Scotland? Who were the druids, and the clan? Why had he assumed that she'd been sent to him?

A dragging sound came from the other side of the door, which opened.

Rachel watched as a tall, lanky form appeared

on the threshold. She recognized his dark green eyes and grim expression, but not the copper-red hair. It balanced features too bold and fierce to be handsome, and gave him the look of a large, predatory feline.

Evander.

Chapter Four

THE HIGHLANDER'S CLOTHING looked like nothing Rachel had ever seen. His dark leather trousers and light-colored woven shirt had been hand-sewn, and not very well. She noticed patches in several places that were definitely functional instead of decorative. His long hooded cape had several rents in the wool, and his boots looked worn. His weapons were in better shape than his clothes. He carried two polished, sharp-looking daggers tucked in his belt, and a well-made leather harness across his chest. She'd never seen a man look more feral or dangerous, but he didn't frighten her. Everything about him made her feel comforted, and safe.

"You're awake," he said and didn't sound as if he was happy about that. He didn't look it, either.

She glanced past him to see a tall wooden frame that he must have had holding the door shut. Strands of wool had been stretched from its top bar to the bottom. It seemed to be some kind of loom.

"You don't have to barricade me inside here," she said, and cleared her throat as her voice rasped on the words. "I won't try to escape."

"You're no' my prisoner. I but needed to sleep without worrying you would stray from the house." He hesitated before he added, "You'll want something to wear."

She had a vague memory of seeing him toss her ruined clothes in a fireplace.

"Thank you. That would be nice."

Evander frowned, and went over to open an old trunk. He sorted through its contents before he took out a dark brown skirt, a lace-up blue blouse, and a long cummerbund-shaped sash. He looked at them for a long moment before he straightened.

Fiona, forgive me, Rachel heard him say inside her mind.

"You can wear these things." He brought the clothing to her. "I'll make food while you dress."

Once he left, Rachel surveyed the garments, which were all neatly hand-sewn, but had been made for Fiona, who had obviously been curvier and a few inches taller. She managed to get them on and figure out the crude fasteners, but the blouse billowed over the skirt, which dragged on the floor matting. She tucked and folded over the fabrics where she could, securing them with the sash, which she had to double around herself before tying it. Rachel glanced down at herself. God, she looked like a kid playing dress up with great-great grandma's clothes.

Other things around the room hinted at a woman's presence: a pot of dried flower stalks, two handmade cushions embroidered with spiral stitches, long faded ribbons neatly wound around some long wooden spindles, and several pairs of cloth slippers neatly lined up beneath the edge of a tall cabinet. A wooden comb with surprisingly fine teeth sat beside a silver plate that had gone brown with tarnish.

Fiona hadn't just died in this room. She'd lived here.

Without a mirror or brush Rachel couldn't do anything about her hair except work her fingers through the tangles. That was when she discovered that her hair had inexplicably grown out almost to her waist, and while it was still stick-straight it felt much thicker and stronger now. Completely bemused, she wove the heavy length into an untidy braid and looped the end to hold it secure.

The adjoining room appeared to be the main area of the cottage, and the first thing she saw was the big chair by the stone fireplace where she guessed she had fallen asleep on Evander's lap. To the left of the hearth stood two chairs made from tree branches and log slices on either side of a stone table. Rachel felt numb as she approached it, and reached out to touch the green-streaked granite. The pattern of the stone matched exactly her mother's honeymoon table, but it looked much newer, and stood supported by two massive tree stumps. If what Evander had told her was true, then in eight hundred years Rachel's mother would find this table, and her father would buy it, and it would be shipped to California to become part of Avalon.

Rachel knew it might just be a huge coincidence, but it didn't feel like one.

Evander came to join her, and set a small pot of steaming oatmeal on the table.

"I've no milk for the porridge," he said.

"This is fine," she assured him, and saw some wooden bowls, plates and spoons on a nearby shelf. "May I help and set the table?"

He eyed her. "You cannae lift it."

"I mean do this." She picked up two bowls and spoons and placed them by the oatmeal.

Evander said nothing as he portioned out the meal, giving her twice as much as she could eat before filling his own bowl. He then went into the back room and returned with a corked jug and two pottery cups, one of which he filled with a sweet-smelling cider from the jug.

"'Tis called perry," he told her, and offered her the cup.

Rachel cautiously sampled the cider, which tasted of pears instead of apples, and had enough kick to tell her it had been fermented. She handed the cup back to him.

"It's a little too strong for me."

He fetched her a cup of water, and finally sat down to eat.

The oatmeal had been sweetened with honey, which Rachel found delicious, but she ate sparingly as she waited for her stomach to protest. Over the last month she had been feeling nauseated nearly every time she ate. David had insisted on bringing her meals on a tray to her room. He'd also given her a glass of wine every night, assuring her that it would help her sleep. That must have been how he'd been dosing her. Drugs in her food, in her drinks, probably even in her toothpaste.

Rachel looked across the table at Evander, who was watching her intently. "Is something wrong?"

He reached out to flick his fingertip over her cheek, and showed her the tear he'd caught.

"The oatmeal isnae so bad, is it?"

"It's actually very good," she managed to say before her throat tightened. She set down her spoon. "May I ask you something?" Once he nodded, she said, "Why were you in the oak grove last night, Evander?"

"'Tis where I buried Fiona. She was my lady." He nodded at her blouse. "The garments are —were—hers."

Rachel took a sip of water before she continued.

"Was I... How did you know I would be there?"

"I didnae." He stood and walked out into the garden.

Rachel stared at the door Evander had left open. She'd hoped he would tell her something that would explain why she had been brought here, and the reason he'd been planning to kill himself before he'd rescued her. She owed him the truth about her powerful new ability, too, but would he even believe she could read his mind?

She wasn't even sure she believed it.

Rachel went out into the garden, where she found Evander sitting on a bench, staring at a patch of withered white flowers being crowded out by bigger, thorny yellow blooms. He looked just as big and tough and hard-eyed as when she'd first seen him, but she felt a wave of wordless emotion rolling off him that flooded her with regret and grief.

He was thinking of Fiona without words but with memories. Fiona walking through some sort of outdoor market with a large basket on her arm. Fiona, awash in bright sunlight, sitting on a stool and moving a shuttle through a loom. Fiona working in the garden while fat bumblebees buzzed around her. Her name, echoing inside his mind like a mantra: Fiona, Fiona, Fiona.

He'd loved her so much that nothing Rachel said would ever ease his pain. It made her feel a twinge of envy. She had never been loved like that.

"My mother grew roses," she told him as she sat down beside him. The garden looked as if it had once been well-tended, but had been let grow wild for some time. "She raised them in every color, but she liked white the most. She told me once that they were the symbol of true love. I'm sorry that your wife died."

"We never had the chance to marry," he said and met her gaze, his own edged with anger. "Did the gods send you to me, my lady? Or did she?"

"I think you brought me here," she said as she tucked her arms around her waist in an attempt to conceal how much her hands were shaking. "I saw you right after it happened."

"After you crossed over?" he asked.

Rachel shook her head. "After my husband David stabbed me in the back, and buried me alive."

ᎧᏣᏍᎥ

EVANDER WATCHED the rim of the morning sun appear above the ridge. Though it gilded Rachel with pale amber light, its distant warmth did nothing to end her shivering. Evander took off his cloak and draped it around her, tugging the hood up over her head. The moment he touched her he felt his skinwork move under his tunic, and quickly removed his hands.

"I couldnae bring you here, my lady," he told her. "I've no' such powers. You saw me only after I took you from the ground."

"Then who would do this?" she asked. "I don't know anyone here. My husband just wanted me dead."

"You crossed over on the same night I came to the grove, and that I had no' done for weeks. 'Tis no' by chance, I reckon." Evander eyed her. "Why did your husband try to kill you? Is he mad?"

"Just greedy. He wanted my inheritance." Her expression grew bitter. "My father was a very wealthy entrepreneur, like, ah…"

"Nobility?" Evander suggested.

She nodded. "Something like that. David's father worked for mine, and introduced us. I lost

my parents in a fire a few months ago, and I—"
She gave him a stricken look. "Oh, God. While he
was burying me he said he thought about using
fire again to get rid of my body. I think David
murdered them."

He took her cold hand in his. "Tell me everything, lass."

Evander had to clamp down on his temper as
he listened to Rachel describe how her husband
had used and deceived her. He could see that the
death of her parents had left her vulnerable to the
murderous fack, who had obviously used her pain
to manipulate her into marrying him. It made
him wish he had the power to use the grove
portal, so he might travel to the future, find David
Carver, and gut the coward slowly. He would
teach him what justice was brought to men who
destroyed lives to serve their own greed.

As was never done to me.

Shame burned inside him as he thought of
Tharaen Aber, the laird's bodyguard, who had
tried to stop him from running away with Fiona.
He had intended only to wound Aber, but when
his spear had pierced the other man's throat, he
had taken Fiona and left Aber to die. The fact
that they had been old, bitter enemies, or that the

clan would have killed Fiona for serving as a spy for the undead, did not justify what Evander had done.

When Rachel finished, he knew she had every right to go before the druid conclave and demand justice.

"Do you wish vengeance on your husband? It may be had, if you go to your people. I can take you to them."

"It won't change what David did," she said, and hunched her shoulders. "The man I loved doesn't exist. My parents are gone forever. I've lost everything, even the world I lived in. I only wish I knew what to do now."

Evander didn't understand her mercy, but he did her despair. Since losing Fiona he had been wandering aimlessly through each day, desperate to find purpose and meaning in an empty existence. He would have happily fought to his death to kill as many of the bastarts who had violated and forced Fiona to spy for them. He may not have had great affection for females himself, but he loathed men who used their weakness as a weapon against them. If he could use the portal to go to San Diego, and find Rachel's husband, he would skin him alive, and enjoy every moment of it.

"I'm all right, Evander," Rachel said suddenly. "Don't worry, I'll figure out what to do."

The lass had no inkling of the world she had come to. He would have to look after her, at least in the beginning. Perhaps that was why he was drawn to the grove on the same night Rachel had been sent through the portal. The gods wished him to protect her. But why had they chosen him? Surely they knew he had no love for women, and even less since Fiona had died.

Rachel looked so miserable that he feared she might start weeping again. He did not care for women, but to watch one cry was the worst kind of torture. To prevent it, he stood and drew her to her feet.

"Come and walk with me."

Evander led her from the garden out to the old, winding trail that led into the woods. Moss and lichen carpeted the path, and the last of the summer wildflowers painted the grassy slopes with blue, purple and white blooms. Thistledown drifted on the air, catching on their garments before their movements dislodged the floating seeds.

When Evander guided her out of the trees and onto the shelf of rock overlooking the rolling glen, Rachel inhaled quickly and pressed her fingertips to her mouth.

"Fiona named it Splang, for the way the light flashes on the water," he said as he looked out over the shimmering surface of the fairy pool. "The little waterfalls freeze in winter, and then bring fresh meltwater when the thaw comes."

A gray-faced red deer came out of the trees and delicately made its way through the fern to drink from the water's edge, followed by a smaller, white-spotted fawn. They were joined by the rest of their herd, and began grazing on the lush grasses blanketing the banks.

Evander glanced at Rachel, who was staring wide-eyed at the deer. "What do you think of it?"

"I've never seen anything so beautiful," she whispered.

"The water is cold, but on sunny days you can swim, if you dinnae mind the company of trout and greylings," he told her. "The deer can be bold, but I've no' hunted them. Fiona didnae eat so much after we came here."

Rachel stood on one of the flat-topped rocks. "Was she sick?"

"The plague took her from me." The words came out of him ragged and harsh, and he turned away.

"I didn't mean to pry," she said quickly.

Of course she did. All females did.

"I dinnae mind it. What more would you ken? How thin she grew, how any sound made her flinch, how she looked upon me when I wished to comfort her? Or mayhap how she died. How the pox scourged her lovely skin. How she burned with fever after fever until it filled her chest and cut off her air?"

"I shouldn't have asked," she said, her eyes filled with sympathy. "I'm sorry."

Evander didn't want her compassion. "Dinnae be. Fiona was my mistress. Before we came here, I visited her in secret. Men of my clan are no' permitted to have such wenches." He looked back at her. "But I didnae care."

Pain flickered across her face. "You can't choose who you love."

"Love? I facked her, Rachel. I treated her like a hoor, and she loved that. She made me think she loved me." He gave her his back again. "'Twas all a lie. She spied for our enemies, and became my lover so she might use me to find my clan's hidden stronghold."

Her footsteps drew near. "Evander—"

He held out his hand to stop her from coming closer. "Her masters ordered her to capture and kill me, but she exposed herself, and I took her prisoner." He turned around to face her. "I am no' a forgiving man. I hated her for her betrayal. I wanted her to suffer at my hands. I meant to beat her to death, that very day."

Instead of looking outraged or frightened, Rachel simply watched him with her dark velvet eyes.

"And then she told the truth of what she was," he continued. "Her masters had murdered her father, and taken her when she was but a lass of fourteen. They violated her, and then used her fear of more to make her spy for them. 'Twas that, or die an ugly death." He looked down at the grazing herd. "When she was ordered to end me, she couldnae bring herself to do it, so she planned an escape. She meant to take me with her to Britannia, and keep me as husband."

"She really did love you," Rachel said softly.

"Aye," Evander said and finished the sordid

tale by telling Rachel what he had done to free Fiona, and how he had left Tharaen Aber to die. "I knew I couldnae save his life," he added, "and to stay would have ended ours. So I took Fiona and fled. We remained in hiding for a time, and then came here. A year later I buried her in the grove."

Rachel came a step closer. "Evander, please, look at me."

"I am a traitor and a murderer." He didn't want to see the disgust on her face.

"You loved her." She came around him, the hood falling back from her face as she looked up at him. "My parents might still be alive if I hadn't fallen in love with David. Does that make me a killer, too?"

"Dinnae be daft." He felt a yank, and glanced down to see his tunic in her fist.

"You think I couldn't kill?" The softness vanished from Rachel's face. "My husband did unspeakable things to me, but that's nothing compared to what he did to my parents. The two people I loved most in the world died horribly. David found a way to set fire to their bedroom while they were sleeping. He burned them alive, Evander."

He covered her hand with his. "Lass, dinnae torment yourself."

Rachel released her grip on his tunic. "I can't go back to my time, because if I do, he's dead. I'll kill him. I'll take a knife and stab him in the heart." Her chin started to tremble. "I've never wanted to hurt anyone in my life. This is what he's done to me."

Pulling her into his arms should have felt awkward, but once again holding her felt as natural as breathing. Evander felt her tension ease, and his own anger and shame dwindle. That she would understand his regret, and show him kindness instead of contempt, baffled him. He understood the cold fervor of her hatred for her coward of a husband, and would even hold him down so she could skewer him.

"Aren't you going to tell me that with time I'll get over it, and forgive him?" she muttered.

"Why should I do that?" he countered. "A knife to the heart is wiser. If you do, then he'll no' harm another lady."

The pleasure of having her so close spread through Evander. He could blame the many months of solitude he'd spent here, but it seemed more than that. Simply touching Rachel made him feel stronger and surer, as if she were somehow steadying him.

The gods desire balance in all things, but the spirits cannot, his tribe's shaman had told him on his Choosing Day. *If you offer yourself to the war spirit, and it takes you, you will never again know peace.*

He is the finest fighter in the tribe, Evander's father had snapped at the old healer. *Do the work and leave the tranquility to the women.*

"Thank you," Rachel said, sighing into his tunic.

A wreck of a man like him would only bring her more grief, Evander thought, and abruptly released her.

"'Twill be well, my lady. When you have rested I will take you to a druid settlement."

"Wait," she said, fear etching her pale features. "Why can't I stay with you?"

Now that she knew what he had done, she should have been eager to leave him, not afraid to.

"I am not fit to be with you, my lady. The druids are your people. You belong with them."

"I don't know them, and I don't want to go to them." Her dark lashes swept down. "If we were brought together for some purpose, shouldn't we find out what it is first?"

He felt a curious pleasure to know she preferred him over the magic folk, as if she'd given him a boon. Still, he could not look after her, not as hurt as she was. She needed careful tending.

"The druids willnae harm you. They can show you how to live in this time, teach you what you are, and what you may do. I cannae help you with that, lass. I'm Pritani, no' druid kind."

"I have nothing to go back to but a first degree murder charge, so I'd rather stay here. I'm not completely helpless, you know. I'd be happy to clean, and garden, and cook for you." Her cheeks pinked. "If you'll teach me how. I'm a very fast learner, so it won't take long. Please?"

In that moment Evander wanted to kiss her pretty mouth, and carry her back to his bed, and show her exactly how she could please him. As young and sensitive as she was, he knew he could drive her wild with delight. He also knew that if he kept her at the cottage, in time they would likely become lovers.

Yet she had been cruelly used by her husband, while he had buried his shattered heart with

Fiona. But what if he lost his temper with her, as he had with Kinley Chandler? The laird's lady had been a soldier. Rachel had been nobility. He knew nothing of her world, nor she his.

"You shouldnae be here with me," he said finally. "Nor I with you."

"I won't try to take Fiona's place," Rachel said and touched his sleeve. "I know I can't. But we can be friends, and keep each other company. It has to be better than you living alone, or me with a bunch of people I don't know."

"You dinnae ken me," he reminded her.

She smiled for the first time, and it transformed her features from lovely to breathtaking. "Then give me a chance to."

In that moment Evander could not have denied her anything. Nor did he want to let her go and return to his wretched solitude.

"Aye, so I shall. Only you mustnae leave the cottage unless I am with you."

Below them a large red stag uttered a stuttering call, and the rest of the deer herd followed him as he fled into the trees. Evander saw the cause for their hasty retreat when a small, dark-furred marten bounded up to the edge of the pool. It drank until it had drenched the amber bib of fur under its pointed face. With a flick of its long, bushy tail, it bounced over to a pine to scamper up into the branches.

Rachel watched it until it disappeared. "That was adorable, whatever it was."

He could tell her that the sinuous, furry assassin had been revered by the Talorc tribe, who emulated its supple grace and swift, lethal strikes in their fighting styles. Martens were night hunters, and his people believed that seeing one in the daylight meant the gods had bestowed special protection over beholders. But Rachel was not Pritani, nor did she know he was an immortal who had lost his tribe a thousand years ago.

The realization hit him like a hammer to the chest. Throughout his long existence Evander had always been regarded as an unrivaled warrior, but that had never endeared him to anyone. During his first, mortal life his tribe had used him like the terrible weapon he was. The warrior's life had hardened him to such a grim, joyless being that his betrothed had run off with another. After being reborn as an immortal, Evander had been respected by the McDonnel Clan for his talents, but never well-liked. He imagined even Fiona had loved him in spite of who and what he was. He'd never known the pleasure of being ordinary, and accepted, or appreciated for anything other than his ability to kill.

Yet Rachel knew nothing of him. With her, Evander could simply be a man.

"'Twas a marten," he told her, smiling a little. "They are the best hunters in the forest."

Chapter Five

L IKE A ROMAN statue washed ashore after a disastrous wreck, Quintus Seneca stood on the plateau atop the Isle of Staffa, and watched as a Ninth Legion ship dropped anchor in the distance. He could see the roughness of the waves churning against the lapstrake hull, now so heavily tarred that the long staggered planks looked like mere ripples. The enlarged, reinforced holk was bulky and unbeautiful from stem to stern, but it easily carried three hundred of his men. He had personally directed the refitting of the cabins and lower decks to protect the undead patrol crews from the lethal rays of daylight.

"'Tis the *Raven*," Ermindale said. The silver-haired marquess beside him snapped his fingers.

One of their escort trotted over to him. "Send out dories for the patrol, and ready fresh thralls for them."

The centurion slapped his forearm across his chest and bowed over it. "At once, Prefect."

Quintus could not fault Ermindale as his second in command. The marquess had taken to his duties with as much relish as he had surrendering his mortality to become an eternal blood-drinker. While he was Scottish, the man had an aura of authority that was undeniable. He also presided over the legion without sentiment or malice, which was rare even among Romans. If not for the transport and sanctuary provided by his slaver ships and vast estates in the north and south, the Ninth Legion might have been exterminated by now. Quintus didn't trust Ermindale, but as long as he continued to prove resourceful, he would keep him as his second.

As they returned to the entrance of their cavernous lair, Quintus saw that the sentries watched Ermindale closely.

"You are making the guards nervous, Prefect."

The marquess smirked. "I have since Ficini departed this earth."

The fact that Ermindale had slain his predecessor to attain his position did not tarnish him in the men's eyes. Such deadly ambition had always been a hallmark of Roman nobility. That the marquess had done so without permission, however, remained a silent point of contention.

"Try not to murder anyone else," Quintus said mildly. "We yet remain at half-strength."

Beneath the island's grassy plain the legion had extended the tunnels and caverns to create a new stronghold. In another month it would be ready to house the remainder of the legion. At Ermindale's southern estates his former slaves were in the process of being turned into undead and trained as replacements for the Romans who had fallen during the northern siege. Once the new troops were brought to the Isle of Staffa, Quintus could initiate the final phase of their plan to remove the only obstacle between the legion and rule over Scotland: the McDonnel Clan.

Inside the lair Quintus walked through the passages lined with naturally-formed basalt columns that lent the air of a temple to the underground complex. Mortal thralls, busy with the daily work of looking after their undead masters, smiled and nodded as they passed. A dozen smiths they had abducted from their villages now happily forged new blades in the armory. A line of maids snatched from their noble households giggled as they carried mounds of washing into the laundry. The smells of cooking drifted from the huge kitchen that prepared daily meals for the island's thralls, all of whom had been converted with the new method of enthrallment Quintus had discovered.

Drinking only a small amount from the veins of the undead, and having their wounds healed with a smear of undead blood, turned ordinary mortals into absolutely devoted, willing slaves.

"I will join you and the men shortly," Quintus said to the marquess, and left him to enter his private chambers.

Cases of books taken from monasteries and great estates lined the stone walls. Finely-knotted carpets covered the rough floors. A few candles illuminated the darkness, enough to see the voluptuous body reclined on the curtained bed. A silky fall of long, bright golden hair was all that adorned Fenella Ivar's translucent skin. When Quintus stood over her she opened her light blue eyes and smiled.

"Have you need of me, milord?" she asked in her dulcet voice.

He sat down beside her, and took one of her strong, square hands in his. Her palm and fingers still felt rough from the years she had spent laboring as a dairy maid, but he liked how they felt on his cold flesh.

"Not now, my dear," he said. He was becoming exceedingly fond of the maid, and that seemed a dangerous weakness, especially when he saw how pale she had grown. "You should dress and go have a meal."

"If that is your wish, milord," she said. But she pushed herself upright, pressing her large breasts against him. "You ken what I hunger for."

Quintus felt how cold and clammy her skin was, and kissed her brow. "Eat something, and I will join you again later."

He left Fenella to meet the patrol from the ship in the large cavern serving as their command center. He found them and the marquess gathered around a broad map table.

"We bring news, Tribune," Cicarus, the optio commanding the patrol, said. "As we returned to the ship we picked up the blood scent of an injured mortal female. We spotted her in the arms of a highlander, here." He pointed to a spot on the map. "But they escaped before we could

capture them. We found a half-dug pit in the
grove that contained her blood, but lost the scent
of the woman at a nearby stream."

"Mayhap you interrupted a murder," Ermindale suggested sourly.

"That grove was where the fire-throwing
witch murdered Tribune Lucinius," Quintus said
and frowned at the optio. "Describe the highlander to me."

"Tall, red haired, and dressed in dark
garments. He wore no tartan." Cicarus thought
for a moment. "He did carry a bundle of spears
harnessed to his back."

"That was the McDonnel traitor, Evander
Talorc," Quintus said softly. "What else?"

"We recovered this from the grave."

The optio handed him a small, soiled white
rectangular pouch hanging from a finely-wrought
chain.

Quintus fiddled with the clasp until it opened,
and removed a small folded object filled with
strange colorful cards made of some slick mater-
ial. One of them bore a miniature portrait of a
dark-haired beauty, and tiny words printed all
over the card.

"California Driver License." He touched the

raised lettering of the signature under the portrait. "Rachel Ingram." The numbers and letters made no sense to him, so he showed the card to Cicarus. "Is this the woman?"

"I believe it is, Tribune." The optio sniffed the card. "And it smells of her."

Talorc had disappeared along with Fiona Marphee, Quintus's most valuable mortal spy, more than two years past. Rumors that the former McDonnel seneschal had betrayed his clan for his lover had slowly spread over time, but no one had seen them since the destruction of the Ninth's original lair.

"I want all of the men to see this," Ermindale said, taking the portrait card from Quintus and handing it to Cicarus. "Every patrol is to search for this woman and take her alive."

The optio bowed. "As you command, Prefect."

Quintus waited until Cicarus left before he said, "We need Talorc, not a female."

"If he wished her dead, he would have left her for our men," the marquess said. "That he took her away shows she has some value to him. Perhaps she is his new lover. If he betrayed his clan for the last wench he facked, then he will again. A branded traitor like Talorc may even choose to ally himself with us against them."

Now he could see the marquess's reasoning, and yet felt a surge of anger. Ermindale had no regard for women, and if they succeeded in capturing Rachel Ingram, would likely enthrall her to serve as his personal whore.

"Talorc kens where Dun Aran is," Ermindale said. He smiled as if he'd been given a gift. "We'll double the patrols, and alert our mortal spies. And we'll want more of those, by the way."

"Try to enthrall some men as well as women," the tribune advised his prefect.

Quintus discussed the areas to search with the men, and then left Ermindale to arrange for the new patrols while he returned to his chambers. He saw that his bed stood empty, but when he drew closer he found Fenella sprawled naked and unconscious on the rug. He pressed his fingers to her throat, and found her pulse weak and fluttering. Her lips and fingernails looked bluish, and her flesh felt cold as ice.

"Milord," she gasped. "I cannae…breathe."

He had killed enough mortals to know she was dying, yet he had been so careful not to take too much of her blood. This was the work of another.

Her life would end in minutes, unless he gave her immortality. But no female had yet been turned and made undead. He had vowed to avoid it at all cost.

As he lifted her to the bed, he saw fresh bite marks on her throat, marks that could not be his. A dull rage rose up inside him.

"Who did this to you?"

She murmured something unintelligible, and went limp.

Whoever had done this thing would suffer for it, but in this moment he had to save her, which meant feeding her his blood before her heart stopped, and beginning the process of turning her. He raised his wrist to his mouth, biting into his own flesh to make himself bleed.

He pressed the wound against her lips. "Drink," he said softly. "Yes, my sweet. Like that, my love."

Chapter Six

LAIRD LACHLAN MCDONNEL watched the heavy bank of clouds advancing on the stark ridges of the Black Cuillin mountains. The denseness of the approaching storm fractured the sun into huge shards of white light that stabbed at the shadowy depths of Loch Sìorraidh, while far-off lightning flashed ever brighter. Such tempests were nothing new on the Isle of Skye, or to his clan of immortal highlanders, but today the laird felt a peculiar menace in the air. His serpent spirit also felt it, for he could feel the ink of his skinwork twitching under his garments.

Something was coming, and it had nothing to do with the weather.

"Here you are," said a sweet, familiar voice.

The tall, slender figure of his wife, Kinley, emerged from the upper hall archway and came to stand beside him at the edge of the curtain wall walk. "Ovate Lusk has just arrived and is asking to speak with you. He looks worried, so it's probably not good news, but he didn't bring Bhaltair Flen, so it's likely not too horrible." She slipped her arm around his waist. "Something wrong?"

"Mayhap, but I cannae put name to it." He glanced down at the grimy condition of her sparring garments. "You've been tussling with Diana again."

"No, she kicked my ass again," Kinley corrected, and sighed. "I'm a combat-trained Air Force officer who did three tours in the sand pit, and I keep getting stomped by a cop who worked missing persons." She rolled the top of her right arm as if it were sore. "It's embarrassing."

Lachlan rubbed her shoulder for her. "Diana Burke is the tallest, strongest female I have ever seen, and she is married to the largest, strongest, fastest warrior in the clan."

"Oh, now I get it," she said. Tiny streaks of white in his wife's vivid blue eyes flashed like the distant storm. "You're having Raen train her."

"Aye, my love, but no' to defeat you," he said

quickly as she thumped him with her fist. "I've tasked them both with leading warbands to search for the undead on the mainland. Diana may be the finest tracker we've ever had, but she's wanting in other areas."

"So our cop needed to learn how to fight like a highlander." Kinley's glare softened. "Well, she does now, so you can tell Raen to teach me all those fiendish Pritani moves."

"Ah, but he has many duties as our seneschal." He tugged her closer. "And my Pritani moves are more wicked."

As he bent his head to kiss her smiling lips, Lachlan once more silently thanked the gods for the gift of his wife. Brought back eight hundred years from the future, the first thing Kinley Chandler had done was save his life during a battle with the undead. From that night she had fought him, tempted him, and bewitched him with her sharp mind and uncommon beauty. Yet it was the wounded spirit in her that had called out to his own. Passion and love had brought them together and helped them to heal one another.

When the kiss ended she trailed her fingertips over his mouth. "Just how wicked, exactly? Like... naked moves?"

"I cannae tell you," Lachlan murmured. "I must teach you in our chambers."

Her expression turned grave. "Uh-oh. I know that look. We might break furniture. Again." She looked around before she whispered, "Well, we've wanted a bigger bed, right? I'll get Neac started building a new one now."

Lachlan chuckled and held Kinley close. Since they had married, time no longer weighed on him as it had before. He no longer had to face eternity alone. She had also been made immortal, thanks to her enormous courage during a horrific battle with the undead. Without hesitation she had sacrificed herself to kill the legion's fanatical tribune, and stop the slaughter of hundreds of druids. The moment he'd seen her use her power of fire to burn herself and the tribune to death, it had driven him mad.

"I think the snake heard us," Kinley said, and slipped her hand into his collar to caress the inked serpent's head on his shoulder. "Maybe it'll help you teach me."

"That is not what it wishes to do to you, my lady."

He heard the trod of sandals on the stones and looked over his wife's pale gold mane to see a druid ovate in dark robes approaching them. Cailean Lusk appeared to be nothing more than a slim, dreamy-eyed boy, when in truth he had already lived seven lifetimes.

At that moment large rain drops began pelting the walkway, as if the gods themselves wept.

"My lord, my lady," Cailean said and bowed quickly. "I dinnae wish to intrude, but I am sent on a matter most urgent. Our allies report a disturbance in the sacred grove. 'Tis possible that another female from a future time crossed over last night, but she has disappeared."

Lachlan felt Kinley tense, and nodded. "We'll speak inside."

The three of them retreated into the stronghold, where the laird led his wife and the druid to his tower chamber. Margret Talley, the castle's chatelaine, intercepted them as she brought in a tray with mugs of hot spiced cider and a platter of fruit, cheese and oat cakes.

"The magic folk forget to eat, and ye've no' yet breakfasted, milady," the old woman said as she placed the tray on the table, and gave Kinley's sparring garments a narrow look. "Once ye're finished scheming, I'll send up hot water for yer bath, and a proper gown." She bobbed before Lachlan and left.

"That woman won't be happy until *I'm* the largest female in the clan," Kinley complained, but scooped up a wedge of cheese and a cake as she perched on the window sill.

Lachlan handed Cailean a mug, and watched him warm his hands on the sides.

"You've been having mortals guard the groves, then?" Lachlan said.

The druid gave him a wary look. "No' guard, my lord. After Mistress Burke crossed over unnoticed, the conclave thought it prudent to keep watch for others." He took a sip of the steaming cider before he added, "This traveler didnae appear in the grove. She was dug out of the earth."

"What?" Kinley got to her feet. "She was buried?"

"'Twould seem so," Cailean said. "We fear something went awry during her crossing. A cloaked man came to the grove just before she arrived. He took her from the ground, and carried her off into the woods. Neither has been seen since."

Lachlan frowned. "He didnae deliver her to a magistrate, or his laird?"

The druid shook his head. "A patrol of undead pursued them, and searched the woods. They didnae find them, but they took something from the grave before they retreated to the hills."

"Sunrise destroys the undead trails, but our tracker can find the two mortals," Lachlan said.

He stepped out into the hall and sent a sentry to summon Raen and Diana. When he returned, he saw his wife examining a dagger with an oddly-shaped wooden handle and a long, sharply-pointed blade.

"Our watchers recovered this knife from the pit in the grove," Cailean told him.

"It's definitely from my time," Kinley said, and held it up to the light from the window. "Fixed blade, double-edged, deep finger choil, palm-centered mass. Not military issue, but professional grade. And I'm seeing traces of blood on the guard and the hilt grooves." She handed it to Lachlan.

He hefted it, surprised by the razor-sharp edges, and how light it felt in his hand.

"Who would carry a knife like this?"

"It's not a utility blade, and it's a bit too long

for close in-fighting," Kinley said and thought for a moment. "I'm not sure. Covert attack dagger, maybe." She saw how the druid was staring at her and grimaced. "Hey, I was combat search and rescue. We didn't kill people. We saved them."

A brisk knock sounded before the Abers came into the chamber. A towering mountain of muscle, the former bodyguard immediately scanned the interior, while his tall, red-headed goddess of a wife sized up the three occupants with her shrewd gaze.

"My lord, my lady. Ovate Lusk." The lightning bolts inked on one side of Raen's face took on a faint gleam as he regarded the blade in Lachlan's hand. "Trouble?"

Lachlan quickly explained the situation, and as soon as he finished Diana exchanged an intent look with Kinley. Lachlan nodded.

"I ken 'tis likely we have another visitor from your time," he said. "That a man came to take her from the grove, and the undead then pursued them, are vexing."

Raen regarded Cailean. "He wasnae a druid?"

"No' from any settlement near the grove, Seneschal." The other man hesitated before he said, "The man has visited the grove several times before last night. He leaves white flowers in the center of the stones."

"Is that where he dug her out of the grave?" Diana asked, and when the druid nodded she turned to Raen. "We need to go have a look at the scene."

"Aye, and from there I wish you to track them," Lachlan told her. "We must find the lass who crossed over before the legion does. Once you have located her, bring her back to Dun Aran."

"And the man who took her?" Raen asked.

"Him, too," Kinley said. "I want to know how he knew she was coming."

"And how he spirited her away so quickly," Cailean put in. "'Tis difficult enough for a mortal to elude the undead, but to do so while carrying a lady is quite a feat."

Lachlan felt a pang of suspicion, and frowned. "Take Tormod and Neac with you, and arm yourselves."

"The undead cannae attack during the day," the big man told him. "But they may send their mortal thralls to fight us. We will be watchful, my lord."

After Diana and Raen left, Cailean said, "Thank you, my lord. Might I remain here at the castle until the lady is recovered? I wish to report back to the conclave when we have news of her."

Lachlan suspected he also wanted to see the woman so he could ferret out the reason for her crossing over, and what powers she might possess. They also might need his help if the traveler was badly injured, as the dagger from the future suggested.

"Aye," Lachlan said. "See Meg and she'll arrange a room for you."

Chapter Seven

DIANA STEPPED OUT of the stream and released her husband's hand as she wiped her face and squeezed the water out of her braid of gilded copper hair. "I always love the ride, but getting drenched in the process, not so much."

"Ask Cailean to teach you the drying spell," Raen said as he shook himself off, spattering her with more droplets. "He likes you."

"Oh, sure. The same way I like Meg's fish and raisin pie." She turned to watch Tormod Liefson and Neacal Uthar surface as transparent, watery versions of themselves, solidify back into their corporeal forms, and wade out of the stream. "But he's not my only druid pal." Once they joined her and Raen, she murmured a few ancient words under her breath.

Raen grinned as a sudden whirlwind of air blasted the four of them, drying their clothes and hair.

"I wondered what you and Bhaltair Flen talk of when he visits."

"Yeah, well, he's been trying to talk me into going to druid school," Diana said and rolled her eyes. She walked up to the edge of the woods with Raen. "He's always 'tissing me about how it's on me to develop my gifts. You should hear him. 'Tis your duty, Diana. 'Tis your destiny. 'Tis what the gods expect. Like my tracking mojo's not good enough anymore."

"You couldnae be a druidess, Red," Tormod told her as he shook back his white-blond mane before squinting at her with his pale blue eyes. "'Twould require you to wear a great, hot robe while you gather weeds and buss trees and such."

"Aye, and leap into the body of a newborn each time you die," Neac said as he hefted his favorite double-headed axe and rested the shaft on one of his roof-beam shoulders. "Imagine poor Raen with a bairn for a wife until you grow breasts again."

"Thanks for that visual, Chief," Diana said while she studied the labyrinth of old, gnarled oaks, and spotted a faint trail of sparkling green light that the highlanders couldn't see. "Okay, I've got them." She turned to look at the other side of the stream. "That's weird. They come right up to the water, and then disappear." She glanced at her husband. "Maybe they walked upstream from here to disguise their scent from the undead."

Raen exchanged a hard look with his clansmen.

"That wouldnae erase blood scent," Raen said. "Show us where they walked, Diana."

She led them into the woods as she followed the trails. They stopped and pooled a short distance away, where Tormod pointed out one set of hoof prints in the soil.

"The mount was shod," he said and crouched down to examine the marks closely. "Looks to be iron, forged in the old way."

Neac rubbed a big hand over the back of his bald head. "No' a villager's horse, then." He regarded Raen. "I ken what you're thinking, Seneschal, but it cannae be. The man was many things, but no' a fool."

Raen uttered something in their ancient

Pritani language that Diana thought might be a contrary opinion.

"All of our mounts are back on the island," Tormod said. "So unless there were mounted raiders come to rescue the wench, then aye, it can be and probably is."

"Boys," Diana said, folding her arms. "You're talking over my head again. You know how it harshes my mellow when you do that. So what gives?"

"Naught that can be proven yet," her husband told her, his jaw set and his body language screaming ready to rumble. "Please, show us the rest."

She would have gotten cranky right then, but something in the way all three men looked suddenly and lethally serious told her to put the impending tantrum on hold.

"Sure," she said. "This way."

Diana followed the trails as they wound through the trees and into the grove clearing. The two remained entwined all the way into the center of the carved, bullet-shaped ancient stones, where they forked at a ragged-edged, shallow pit in the ground. Once the trails split she could see their colors: bright gold, which spilled into the grave, and a very dark blue that continued alone to the other side of the grove.

"Holy crap," she muttered as she scanned the ground in front of her. She approached the pit and dropped down to run her fingers through the golden light. "This one is a druid, or is like me and Kinley. There's a lot of blood soaked into the soil here, too." She glanced over at the other, darker trail, and nodded at it. "That one is not undead or mortal. I don't know what he is, but the trail is almost black."

"Search the entire grove," Raen told the men before he knelt down beside her. "Why would she bleed after crossing over? The portal should have healed her."

Diana realized what had happened and rubbed her brow. She rarely thought about her life as a detective for the Missing Persons Unit of the San Diego Police Department, but she'd seen too many pits like this to mistake it for anything else.

"It did heal her," she said. "I think she was attacked in my time, not here. Whoever tried to murder her must have buried her alive. She came here because they put her in a sacred grove on that side."

"Gods, no," Raen said as he drew her to her feet and held her for a moment. "And when she woke?"

Diana nodded. "She was still in the ground. It's not that deep, so she may have been able to punch a hand through the soil." Moving to the side of the pit, she inspected the disturbed earth, and pointed to a deep gouge. "There, that's about where her right arm would be. If the guy came to drop his flowers, like Cailean said, he would have seen it. His trail stops here. He must have helped dig her the rest of the way out."

Her husband leaned over to tug something out of the soil, and unearthed a large, H-shaped object. As he shook the dirt from it, Diana saw that it had been carved from a single piece of wood, and depicted two circles with a stylized letter Z on its side between them. On the underside two leather straps had been fixed parallel to each other.

"What is that thing?" she asked him.

"A buckler. The Pritani carried them as shields into battle, and carved them with their spirit symbol so that other tribesmen would ken them." As Tormod and Neac joined them, Raen handed the shield to the chieftain. "He left this in the grave."

The Viking uttered a sour sound. "So he's mad as well as a fool." He saw Diana's expression and tossed out his hands. "If you willnae tell her then I shall. 'Twas Evander Talorc who came and took the wench, Red. The symbol on the buckler, 'tis his war spirit."

She regarded her husband. "This would be the Evander who speared you through the throat so he could run off with the undead spy gal?"

"The same," Raen said and took her by the arm. "We will travel through the stream until you pick up their trail again." When she tugged free of his grip he glared at her. "There is no' a moment to waste."

"Your face is turning into a laser show," she said, and tapped the glittering white-silver ink on his taut cheek. "Their trails aren't going anywhere. You know the drill. We need to report it to the laird first, tell him Talorc is involved, and see how he wants us to proceed. If he says track them, then we come right back and do that. It'll only take a few minutes."

"I agree with Aber," Tormod said. "Evander

may lead the undead to siege the stronghold any time he wishes to attack us."

"The man has been gone from us for years now, Viking," Neac chided. "If he meant to bring the enemy to our walls, he wouldnae have waited this long."

As they squabbled over what Evander may or may not have done, Diana said softly, "Raen, why are you so hell-bent on chasing Talorc?"

"Evander hates females," Raen said flatly. "Before he betrayed the clan he attacked Lady Kinley twice—"

"Now, lad," Neac interrupted. "'Twasnae the case." He addressed himself to Diana. "I've no love for Talorc, no' since he clouted Kinley from behind when first she came to us. He claimed he thought she might harm the laird. The second time she challenged him to fight her in the lists. The laird stopped the bout to spare Evander's pride."

"Aye, for Kinley would have won," Tormod put in.

"Enough," Raen bellowed, and then closed his eyes for a moment. "'Twas my lack of action that permitted Talorc to do this, Diana. I didnae pursue him after he escaped with Fiona Marphee.

Had I sought proper justice, he wouldnae have been here to steal this poor lass from her grave."

"Fine, it's all your fault," she said and smiled at him. "We're still going back to Skye and tell Lachlan about this." She picked up the buckler, and noticed the color of the soil caught in the front carving. "He didn't leave this in the grave recently. It looks like it's been buried here for a while. And see the red dirt? That's blood. The woman who crossed over last night landed on top of it."

Raen went still. "Fack me."

"They always put the bucklers beneath their heads," Tormod said. "Like a bed pillow." He eyed her. "There was another here, Red. One Evander put in the ground, I reckon. 'Twas why he brought the posies."

"I don't understand," Diana said. "Another what?"

"Lady," Neac said and sighed. "'Tis an old Pritani custom. Men of our tribes buried their shields with their wives, to protect them in the afterlife until they could join them. Evander buried Fiona here."

Chapter Eight

RACHEL CARRIED HER morning brew out into the garden, where she sat to watch the sunrise paint the sky. Walls of mist drifting across the ridges and slopes painted the landscape with a dreamy whitewash, adding magic to the lovely view. Birds came out to sing to her, their songs unfamiliar but the cacophony endearing.

She took a sip from her mug, and smiled at the dark, sweet flavor. She didn't miss coffee at all, thanks to Evander's dandelion root tea, and she'd quickly grown to love using honey instead of sugar. Had it been only a week since she'd arrived in this strange, beautiful land? Without clocks and watches and computers Rachel was losing all sense of time—and it didn't bother her in the slightest.

Learning how to live in this simple era without any of the other modern conveniences didn't feel like much of a chore, either, despite the hard work involved. Water had to be hauled from the stream by bucket, while most of the food had to be hunted or gathered. Clothing had to be washed with strong, homemade soap, and hung from low tree branches to dry. While she hadn't yet mastered cooking by fireplace, Rachel could now make simple soups and stews in the iron cooking pot hanging in the hearth. Last night she had baked her first barley-oat bannocks on a flat stone heated by the fire. Evander had only to show her once how to do something. Her cooking had to be all right, as he ate whatever she put on the table without comment.

Rachel sometimes still wondered if this was some version of heaven. Her parents hadn't been religious, but they'd taught her to be open-minded. She'd attended services at churches and temples with friends from school, but no faith had ever attracted her to practice it. Nor did she believe the scientific view that evolution was responsible for everything. She'd always liked the

nebulous thought that there was something more
—something bigger that they couldn't understand
—like some great, hidden design.

Then there was the strange sense of affinity
with the mountains and the woods and land in
Scotland. She felt more at home here than she
had during her entire life in California.

Rachel heard a low groan in her thoughts
and glanced over at the barn. Evander had
insisted she sleep in his bed while he bunked
down with the horses, but with the nights
growing colder that couldn't go on. She rose and
went into the cottage to make another mug of
tea, and brought it out as he came up the path
stones.

"Good– I mean, fair morning," she said and
offered him the mug before she walked with him
into the cottage. "The oatmeal should be ready in
a few minutes. I hope you don't mind, but I added
some cinnamon and apple preserves to it."

Evander glanced at the cooking pot. "'Tis how
you prepare porridge in the future?"

"Sort of. Ours is instant. Well, pretty much
everything of ours is instant, microwaveable, or
pre-packaged."

She went over to check the pot, and then used

a long-handled iron to remove it from the hook over the fire and carried it to the table.

Evander took a ladle from the dish cabinet and portioned out the steaming cereal into the bowls she had set out.

"The frost grows heavier each night," he said. "You shouldnae sit out in the garden too long in the mornings, else you grow chilled."

"I was thinking the same thing about you sleeping out in the barn," she said and sat down across from him and tested the oatmeal. It was fragrant but not too sweet. "If you become ill, I'm in big trouble. I don't know where to find a doctor–"

"I dinnae take sick, and the cold willnae harm me," he said flatly.

In her mind Rachel heard his thoughts just as clearly.

She doesnae believe me, but I cannae tell her that I will never be sick again, or age like her. I willnae allow her to sleep on a stack of blankets on the cold floor. Mayhap I can fashion a cot and put it by the fire. But can I sleep with her in my bed, but ten steps from me?

The carnal desire that accompanied Evander's last thought poured into Rachel, blazing through her breasts and belly to pulse between her thighs.

"I'll get more tea," she said, and quickly went into the kitchen. She poured some water from the urn onto her hand and splashed it on her hot face.

She knew how much he wanted her. Every day she felt it, and often at the oddest moments, such as when she sat and brushed out her wet hair by the fire, or when he watched her while she swept the floor with his reed broom. Despite all that lust, Evander never put his hands on her, or tried in any way to seduce her. She was beginning to think he would keep treating her like a housekeeper forever.

He's waiting on me.

Rachel dried her face with a kitchen cloth, sighing into it. She no longer loved her psychopath husband, but what David had done to her made her reluctant to get more involved with Evander. For one thing, he really didn't care for women. Not in the sense that he preferred men, but more like he had been burned so many times he didn't trust anyone female.

Even if she could overcome his aversion to her gender, there was the stuff going on in his head. Having sex with such an intense man might be thrilling, but some of the strange things he thought made her wary—like just now while they were talking. What kind of man genuinely believed that he would never age or get sick?

"Rachel?"

She whirled around to find him standing just behind her.

"Oh. I'm okay. I just wanted to wash my face." She reached out with the damp cloth to pick up the still-hot handle of the brew pot, but he caught her wrist. "Would you rather have some perry?"

Evander tipped up her chin to study her face. "You're afraid of me now. Why?"

"I don't know," she said without thinking. Really she was more afraid of herself, and the stupid decisions she was quite capable of making. It didn't help that she was totally, hopelessly attracted to him. "I know I can be annoying, and I don't want to make you angry."

"You cannae do that. I'm never no' angry." He smiled a little. "Say what you will."

"Okay. You can't go on spending every night in the barn. You will get sick, Evander, and...you don't have any medicine here," she finished, feeling like an idiot.

"They've a healer in the village," he murmured, and stroked his thumb along her jaw line. "You shouldnae worry on me, lass. I'm never ill."

His mind filled with his need to kiss her, and Rachel's eyelashes fluttered as she stared at his mouth. The desire she felt now wasn't all coming from him, or maybe it was and she simply didn't care. Then she thought of how it had felt to stare up at her new husband as he shoveled dirt on top of her paralyzed body.

She'd wanted David, too.

"I got married seven days ago," she told him, her voice unsteady. "You were still in love with Fiona when you found me. We're both hurting, Evander, and we need more time to heal."

"Aye. We can heal each other."

His eyes darkened, and he bent his head as if he meant to kiss her.

"Not that way," Rachel said and put her palm to his chest. She frowned as she felt his flesh throbbing under the fabric. "Are you having muscle spasms?"

"'Tis my skinwork," Evander said, sounding mystified. He pulled down the collar of his tunic, exposing part of a primitive-looking tattoo. "You rouse my war spirit."

Without thinking Rachel traced one line of the ink, and felt him shudder. She drew her hand away, but he brought it back and pressed her palm over it.

"Never fear to touch me," he told her, his voice going deep and rough. "Your hands are as soft as fine silk, and cool as a spring rain."

"Your skin is so warm," she whispered, her throat so tight she could barely breathe. She took a step back. "This…I don't want you sleeping with the horses anymore. Please, stay in the cottage with me so you don't freeze. That's all I want…for now."

Evander's jaw tightened, but he released her hand and picked up the brew pot.

"I'll fashion a cot. Come and eat, and after you can walk the woods with me."

Relieved that things hadn't gotten out of hand, Rachel quickly finished her oatmeal, and retrieved the gathering basket. Before they left, Evander draped her with his tartan, and folded an edge over her head to form a hood. He pinned it with a spiral of hammered bronze.

She glanced down at the heavy wool. "It won't be that cold today, will it?"

"With the heavy frost comes the wind from

the sea," he told her. "A wee wisp of a wench like you cannae endure it."

"I'm not *that* small," Rachel said as they left the cottage and headed into the forest. "I've also put on some weight since I got here."

"Aye, and I've boots that are still heavier," Evander said and stopped to listen before he nodded to the left. "That way we'll find berries."

Rachel didn't know what he heard, but five minutes later they came upon a huge patch of trees heavily ladened with garnet-red berries. Beneath the branches a small herd of deer had their necks stretched as they nibbled on the lowest clusters.

She was still learning the names of what was edible. "Are they currants?"

"Wild cherries," he said and pointed to a cluster of bushes with much darker fruit near the trees. "And blaeberries there."

As soon as they approached, the herd scattered, making Rachel feel a bit guilty. Her shame faded as soon as Evander plucked a handful of the cherries and offered them to her. She bit into one, and moaned a little over the sweet-tart taste.

They stain your lips red, lovely lass. How I want to kiss that mouth now. Only I wouldnae stop with one kiss. I want a dozen, all tasting of cherry and your own sweetness.

Rachel took the little stone from her mouth before she choked on it.

"How did you know they would be here? Can you hear them growing?"

"I heard the deer," he said and placed a handful of cherries in her basket. "The frost sends them foraging for the last of the summer fruit. They must feed as much as they can so they may grow fat before the snow arrives."

She glanced down at the cherry pit. "We should plant some of these closer to the cottage. Do they bear fruit right away? It would be nice to have cherries in the garden next summer."

He gave her an odd look. "You mean to stay so long here, my lady?"

"Unless you kick me out. I don't have anywhere else to go, remember?"

Before he could suggest otherwise she hurried over to the bushes. Her fingers shook as she began picking the blaeberries, which looked like smaller, blackish versions of American blueberries.

Evander wasn't thinking anything as he gathered the wild cherries, but he kept watching her, and the weight of his gaze made her clumsy. By the time she brought back a skirt full of berries to drop in the basket, her hands dripped with reddish-purple juice. Of course he didn't have a drop of cherry juice on him, which made her feel even more inept.

"I don't suppose there's any water close by," Rachel said as she studied her sticky hands.

"A branch of the river runs beyond those pines. You can wash there."

He picked up the basket and led her deeper into the trees. The river turned out to be much larger and wilder than she expected, and Rachel stopped in her tracks as she surveyed the rushing currents.

"I think this is a bad idea. I am a wee wisp of a wench, and also not a great swimmer." She gasped as Evander swept her up in his arms. "What are you doing?"

"Helping you with it."

He strode down the bank and waded into the water, and stood in the center as he flipped her under his arm and lowered her toward the surface.

Rachel yelped as soon as she immersed her hands in the icy currents, and rubbed them together quickly. When she took them out of the water dark, mottled patches still stained her skin, but all of the sticky juice had been cleaned away.

"Okay," she said quickly.

Evander carried her up to the bank, and lowered her onto a flat-topped rock before he climbed out and sat beside her.

"Better now?" he said.

She felt like hitting him. "Do you realize how dangerous that water is? If you had fallen over, we both would have been swept away."

His eyes caught the sunlight and blazed like burning emeralds.

"I am no' a lousy swimmer, lass."

A rush of memory came back to Rachel, who stared at him as she remembered him ordering her to close her eyes, and hold her breath.

"You went into the stream with me on your horse. You rode *under* the water. How did you do that?"

His mouth hitched. "I told you, you dinnae ken me. Do you wish to?"

Maybe he was hiding something from her, just as she was concealing her mind-reading ability from him. It didn't seem fair to demand an explanation while keeping from him the fact that she could tap into his thoughts any time she wanted.

"That's okay. You saved my life that night. That's all that really matters."

His amusement faded as he stood and rubbed his chest, and then offered her his hand.

"'Tis growing colder. We'll walk back."

Evander didn't say anything more until they reached the cottage, where he retrieved his snares and spear.

"I'll return before dark."

She nodded, and watched him go before she went inside to put away the berries they'd gathered. When she took off his tartan, the bronze spiral dislodged and fell to the floor matting. As Rachel retrieved it, she saw something under the dish cabinet.

The dusty little scroll had been written by a shaking hand in a language Rachel didn't recognize, but the name at the bottom was only too clear: Fiona. Whatever it said, only Evander could translate it. The sudden urge to tear it to pieces shocked her, as did the wave of jealousy that came with it.

Carefully she placed the scroll on the stone table, and went to curl up in Evander's chair. Fiona had lived a miserable life, and had died a terrible death. She had risked her life to protect her lover from her murderous masters. Evander had destroyed his own life to protect her, too. Their love affair must have been pretty epic. Rachel knew all that, and still she felt a needling resentment.

What if the scroll was an old love letter? Hadn't Evander suffered enough?

She glanced over at the standing loom, the one constant reminder of Fiona.

"I don't know if you're haunting this house, lady, but if you are, could you give the guy a break? He still loves you, but he's trying to move on. Let him, okay? Don't you want him to be happy?"

A sharp sound made her jump, but it came from the fireplace, where a log that had cracked in half fell in two glowing white-red pieces.

"And now I'm talking to myself and burning wood," Rachel muttered.

Finally she forced herself to get up and begin the process of making a stew for their evening meal. She pitted two bowls of wild cherries, which she planned to lace with cream and a dash of the sweet red wine Evander liked. She set out the dishes, trying her best to ignore the scroll, and went out to pick the last of the white heather to make a bouquet for the table.

The highlander returned just before sunset with a brace of ptarmigan and two rabbits, which he stowed in the pantry before joining her. As soon as he saw the scroll on the table he stopped in his tracks.

"What is this?"

"I found it under the cabinet," she said and forced a smile as she handed it to him. "I can't read what's written on it, but Fiona signed it."

Evander unrolled it, studied the words and then looked as if he'd been punched in the face. He started to put the scroll down, eyed the bouquet of heather, and grabbed it. He carried the flowers and the scroll over to the fireplace and pitched both into the flames. From the rigid set of his shoulders and the white-knuckled condition of his fists, he was absolutely furious.

How could she do it? Why would she go, and to where? To them? Did she mean to kill or save herself? Did she never love me?

Rachel waited for a few minutes until he calmed down before she went to him.

"What can I do?"

"Naught. 'Twas a farewell letter from Fiona,"

he told her. "She meant to leave me. While I was out hunting she went to the shepherd's farm. He was to drive her down to the village docks so she could buy passage on a ship. Only she found the shepherd and his family dead from plague, and had to return to me. She died before she could try again."

She curled her hand around his. "I knew I should have burned that damn scroll. I'm so sorry."

"She didnae stab me in the back and leave me for dead," he said through clenched teeth. "No, she waited to gut me from her grave."

"Maybe it wasn't you. Maybe she was so afraid of your enemies that she couldn't stay here anymore," she said, and endured his frigid glower. "You said all she did was worry that you would be found. Maybe it got to be too much for her."

Evander went over to Fiona's loom, which he knocked over to the floor. The tremendous crash made Rachel flinch, but then he broke the frame apart with his bare hands. He selected several pieces, which he leaned against a wall, and then grabbed Fiona's yarn basket.

"Go and have your meal while I build my cot," he told her. "I am no' hungry."

Chapter Nine

IN THE DAYS that followed the discovery of Fiona's Dear John letter, Evander barely spoke to Rachel, and spent most of the day hunting. At night he either chopped wood for the fire or worked in the barn on a new saddle he was making. The hollow tree he used to smoke game smoldered around the clock. The woodpile had gone from substantial to mountainous.

Rachel couldn't fall asleep at night until she heard him come in and stretch out by the fire. The cot he had made from the wood frame of Fiona's loom didn't look particularly comfortable, but when she offered to take turns with him sleeping on it, he flatly refused.

Then there were the long nights when she couldn't drift off even after he came in, when he began dreaming. The memories of battles should have been the worst, and in some ways they were, but he was an amazing fighter. Watching through his eyes as he relived countless skirmishes with the clan's enemies, Rachel discovered he could hurl a spear hundreds of yards and hit any target, even one he could barely see.

He often dreamt of a strange, primitive tribe that at first seemed like prehistoric people. But then she began to pick up on the subtle sophistication of their society and tools. Among the tribe he was always a young boy, and never treated especially well. An older man worked him like a slave, and never offered him a kind word no matter what he did. Evander received terrible beatings for even the smallest mistakes, and had to fight with older brothers for food, battles he often lost until he grew bigger.

Rachel tried everything she could to block out his dreams, but there came a night when she was so tired she just closed her eyes and let him take over her mind. He took her to a little village of cottages, where he slipped into one and walked up behind a dark-haired woman at a loom. When she turned around Rachel expected her to be Fiona, and was shocked to see her own face smiling up at Evander. She nearly fell out of bed, and then felt the sensations coming from him that made her nipples bead and her clit throb between her legs.

In his dream Evander sat down with her on his lap, and fondled her as he watched her face. His long fingers soothed her puckered peaks with circling caresses, and then teased them with little pinching tugs. Rachel wriggled on his lap, impatient for more, but then he turned her over his knee and yanked up her skirts.

She felt the hard, stinging slaps on her bottom as he spanked her in his dream, and while it didn't arouse her it made his chest heave and his penis swell. He loved the domination, the dominion over her, and thought she wanted it as much. He dragged her hand to the confined ridge of his member and pressed her palm against it before he scooped her up and carried her to the bed. He flung her onto it face-first before he stood behind her and hauled up her skirts again.

Rachel's back arched off the bed as in the dream he penetrated her with hard, jabbing strokes. It felt so good she had to pull her pillow over her face to muffle her moans. From the dream she felt what he did, and it was exciting her so much in reality she was ready to come. As her body tightened with need, she slipped her hand between her thighs and quickly stroked her clit. When he ejaculated in the dream it triggered her own climax, and she shook so hard the bed bounced against the wall.

The images and sensations came to a sudden stop, and Rachel heard footsteps approaching from the front room. She closed her eyes and didn't move as she felt Evander bending over her.

Oh, God. She still had her hand between her thighs. What if he could see that she'd been touching herself? What would he think of her?

Evander drew the old tartan over her, covering her body with it from toes to neck. He placed one hand on her belly, and then moved it to rest on the hand she had used to stroke herself. He didn't move her hand or touch her himself, but he knew exactly what she'd been doing. He was thinking about it.

No, he was fantasizing about it.

Rachel held perfectly still as Evander started dreaming again, this time fully awake. He imagined pulling aside the coverlet, and twining his fingers with hers to help her rub her hard little pearl. With the other hand he wanted to tug down the loose collar of her night shirt, baring her breasts to his mouth. He wondered how she would taste, and if sucking her breasts and rubbing her clit would make her come in her sleep.

Oh, please, do it.

Just before she opened her eyes and spoke, Evander drew back from the bed, and the fantasy in his thoughts evaporated. Instead of seeing her, he saw an open grave. Shame and self-disgust filled him as he backed out of the room and hurried out of the cottage.

Rachel felt like weeping as his thoughts grew distant and cold. He hadn't done anything wrong. She had. She felt one last blast of emotion from him—relief, as he dove into the icy loch fully-clothed—and then nothing.

She rolled over, her body aching with need, and cried herself to sleep.

Chapter Ten

AS IF HE knew about the fantasy-sharing, Evander grew even more distant, and spent more time away from the cottage than in it. Aware that she was just as much to blame, Rachel focused on maintaining the peace. She tried to make appetizing meals, kept the rooms tidy, and worked on improving her limited sewing skills. While looking for some old cloth she could practice on she found a pair of wooden knitting needles in a basket of spun wool. After asking Evander's permission to use them, she started working on a scarf at night.

"Mom, you made this look so easy," she muttered as she picked up a dropped stitch, and peered at the uneven rows under it. "But at least I didn't forget everything you taught me."

Rachel spent her days collecting the last of the vegetables and herbs from the garden, and taking stock of what they had in the larder and cold pantry. Once the snow came she guessed that they would be cut off from the village, which meant surviving on whatever Evander could hunt or they had stored.

"Suddenly I have a whole new appreciation for squirrels," Rachel muttered to herself.

Once she had gone through all of their stores she felt a lot better about their situation. Thanks to Evander's daily hunts they had enough smoked and salted meat to last for months. She had counted a dozen huge sacks of oats and barley, and ten of the big, hard-rinded cheeses Evander bought from the miller and a dairy in the village. She'd sun-dried all the peas, beans, apples and pears they had left from the garden and gathering, and had immersed the berries in crocks of honey, which he'd told her would keep them from spoiling. He'd woven the tops of the wild garlic they'd gathered and made a large wreath of it. They'd even have some fresh vegetables for a while, as several heads of kale filled one shelf, and bunches of carrots and wild onions filled another bin.

"Definitely enough flower coffee," she said as she checked the sack she'd filled with dried dandelion stalks to roast and make his favorite morning brew.

They'd squirreled away enough food to remain self-sufficient, Rachel decided. What would happen when bad weather arrived, and neither of them could leave the cottage, still troubled her.

She wanted to comfort Evander, and she suspected sex would make both of them feel much better—the fantasy-sharing had been frankly amazing—but that wasn't a reason to become lovers. The image of the grave in Evander's mind made it clear that he was still mourning Fiona. He also openly avoided touching Rachel whenever he was in the cottage.

Obviously the fourteenth century wasn't the ideal time to have unprotected sex, either. She might become pregnant, and the last thing she wanted was to have a baby in a time when half the women who did died in childbirth. That dilemma also made her wonder how he and Fiona had managed to avoid pregnancy.

That night Evander didn't show up at the

cottage until late. He thanked her for the stew she warmed up for him, but looked almost annoyed when she sat down with him.

"May I ask you something?" she said. He only shrugged in reply. "Did you and Fiona plan on having children?"

Evander almost choked, and had to clear his throat twice before he could reply.

"Fiona's mother died giving birth to her, and she feared the same would happen to her. She didnae want them."

Now for the even trickier question. "How do you avoid that in this time?"

"There are potions and herbs," he said, not seeming at all offended now. "Fiona wasnae obliged to use them. I cannae sire a bairn."

Rachel felt a little stunned. "How do you know that you can't?"

Images of violence and death filled his mind before his thoughts turned to a wall of bleak, dark despair.

"'Twas taken from me."

Rachel excused herself, and went to tidy up the kitchen as she tried to process what she had glimpsed. The strongest image had been of groups of Roman soldiers moving along the shore of a lake, and using their short, ugly swords to slash the throats of other men dressed in furs and hides. She couldn't see Evander anywhere on either side, and then she realized why: she had been seeing the event through his eyes. That he had witnessed such a horrific massacre made her feel sick. Had he been injured? Was that why he couldn't father a child?

Evander brought his dishes in to wash them, and then immediately went out to the barn. She considered going after him to talk about Fiona and the letter again, and maybe even find out when he had fought Roman soldiers, but she could feel a strong, constant pulse of frustration coming from him. She didn't know why, but she certainly didn't want to provoke him into losing his temper again.

"So I'll just sit and knit badly for the rest of the night."

Rachel went into the bedroom to retrieve her work basket, but her heart wasn't in it. Instead she warmed a pot of water over the fire and took it into her bedroom to wash.

The process of hauling and heating enough

water to take a real bath was so labor-intensive
that she'd figured out a simpler method based on
how the Japanese bathed in her time. First she
filled three handled jugs with the warm water, and
then stripped and pulled out the low basin she
kept under the bed. Stepping into the basin, she
wet a washcloth and wiped herself down, then
soaped the cloth and scrubbed herself from neck
to ankles. Finally she slowly poured water from
two jugs over herself, rinsing away the soap. The
basin caught all the water she used, and once she
dried her body she used it to wash her feet.

The third jug of water she reserved for
washing her hair, which she did while leaning over
the basin.

Once she had dressed in the linen shirt
Evander had lent her to use as a night gown, she
carried the collected wash water to the privy,
which occupied a tiny room next to the kitchen.
Once she added a scoop of shell lime, she
dumped her bath water into the primitive
commode, which kept that necessity from
becoming too odorous.

After Rachel blew out most of the candles, she
climbed into the big bed, and curled up under

Evander's tartan. Every night it took a little longer for her body to warm the linens. By the time winter arrived she might have to seduce the highlander just so she could share his body heat.

Finally Rachel felt comfortable, and slowly drifted off to sleep.

In the world of dreams she found herself standing on the porch of her parents' beach house in Monterey. Down by the empty boat dock she could see otters cavorting in the water, and smiled a little as she walked down onto the rocky shore. A woman dressed in a flowing dark robe came out of the trees and met her halfway.

"Hello," Rachel said. Though she knew all their neighbors, she didn't recognize the woman. "Are you new here?"

"I just arrived a short time back," the woman said, her Scottish accent sounding almost musical. "'Tis lovely here, by the sea."

Rachel nodded. "Would you like to come in and have some coffee?"

The other woman shook her head. "I'm no' long for this place. I've another to go to soon." She looked past Rachel, and her expression turned grim. "He's come for you, lass."

Rachel glanced over her shoulder, and saw the tall, handsome man she had married striding toward them, his tennis whites stained with blood and filth.

"How did he find me?"

"Och, you've brought him here, havenae you?" the woman said harshly. "You've let him stand between you and the man you can truly love."

"Rache, darling," David Carver shouted, and spread out his arms. "Where have you been? I've been looking for you."

Her stomach knotted as she saw the long, bloody knife he held in one fist. She tried to run, but her legs wouldn't move.

"You get away from me, David."

"Can't do that, babe," he chided, and picked up his pace to a fast trot. "I need your billions. I need you dead. Why aren't you rotting in the ground yet?"

Rachel looked down to see her legs turning into tree trunks, and her feet sprouting roots that spread out and sank into the soil.

"That man stole your family and your wealth and your life," the robed woman said. "Will you give him your heart as well?"

In another moment he would be on top of her, and Rachel couldn't tear her eyes from him.

"No. He took everything from me."

"No' all. Give him what I never could, lass." The woman retreated back into the trees.

Rachel wrenched at her legs, but now she had become an oak tree from the waist down.

"Go ahead," she told her husband as he reached her. "I'd rather die than feel you touch me again, you son of a bitch."

"Is that any way to talk about my mother? Come on, Rache. You're my wife, at least until death do us part." He caressed her cheek before he moved around behind her, and touched her back. "So please, just shut up and die."

"Go to hell, David."

As the tip of the knife touched her back Rachel finally uprooted herself and fell forward, plunging into a cold darkness. She collapsed onto a woven mat, her whole body shaking, and then a door flung open and strong hands lifted her. She smashed her fists against him as she fought to get free, and then he put her on the bed and wrapped his arms around her, controlling her struggles.

"Rachel, 'tis me," he said and brushed her hair back from her face. "I have you."

She froze, her eyes adjusting to the darkness enough to see Evander's face. He had her pressed against his bare chest. It felt so good to be touched again she almost wept.

"Evander," Rachel said, her voice shaky. She slid her hands up around his neck and pressed her cheek against his shoulder as she tried to control the tremors of fear racking her body. "Oh, god, I had the worst nightmare."

"'Tis over now." He eased her back against the pillows. "I'll fetch some wine. 'Twill help calm you."

"Please," she said and clutched his arm. She wriggled over to make room for him. "Don't leave me alone."

Though he hesitated, Evander eventually stretched out beside her, folding her in his arms, and pulling her atop his chest.

"What did you dream? Was it about your husband?"

She nodded, and as her cheek rubbed against his tattoos she felt a shimmer of heat bloom against her skin.

"David was going to stab me in the back again. I couldn't get away. My legs turned into trees and rooted themselves." She realized how ridiculous that sounded, but at least he didn't laugh at her. "Do you have nightmares like that?"

"No' since you came." The big hand stroking her back moved up to rub the back of her neck. "I do dream of you now and again."

She certainly knew that, but she couldn't admit it. Rachel lifted her head to look at him, but the darkness hid his expression.

"What happens in your dreams?"

"This."

He tugged her up and brought her lips to his.

❦

RACHEL HAD FORGOTTEN how much she missed kissing. David had preferred to hug her or press his lips to the top of her head or the back of her hand. The last time she'd been kissed properly had been during her college days, when she'd sneak her boyfriend into her dorm room for a furtive make-out session before her roommate came back from class.

Evander didn't kiss like a college boy.

He nudged her lips apart for his tongue and tasted her, and then rolled over, tucking her under him as he cradled her face and razed her mouth.

He kissed her as if it might be the last time he ever did, with so much passion and intensity that it felt like they were already having sex. She felt a flush burn down her throat and into her breasts, which throbbed frantically against the solid wall of his chest. When he shifted against her she parted her thighs, and groaned into his mouth as she felt the press of his thick, hard erection.

"Aye," he said as he lifted his head. "Like that I kiss you, over and over again, until you shiver under me as you do now."

Was she trembling? All she felt was heat and hard man on top of her, and the hot, dark smell of him was better than chocolate.

"You should dream for us both." *Again,* she added silently.

He touched her lips with his fingers, tracing the damp curves.

"'Tis only how it begins. When I've stolen the breath from you, I strip you bare and put my hands on your lovely little breasts."

If he didn't do that soon Rachel thought she might explode into climax just from the kissing.

"Would you…show me how you do that?"

Evander tore open the old shirt, exposing her bare breasts and the tight beads of her nipples.

She arched her back as he caressed one mound and then the other, cupping one to knead the weight of her while he teased her peak with his circling thumb. His hands felt so good on her that she went completely wet between her thighs.

"Your soft skin against my hot flesh makes me honest," he muttered, fondling her as he watched her face. "While I caress you, I tell you of the desires I've hid from you."

Rachel felt a pang of guilt. She knew what he wanted, without him saying a word, but that confession could wait a little longer. She wanted to hear him say it.

"What are they?"

"That you torment me so sweetly," Evander said, his voice going deep. "That I grow hard whenever I smell the sweetness of you, or hear your laughter, or watch the candlelight dance in your eyes. How much I long to see you naked and eager for me, here in this bed. The way I want to lick your pretty little quim before I put myself in you. Then to work in you long and hard, until you take your pleasure, and I flood you with my come."

Rachel moved under him until the thick ridge

of his shaft pressed directly against her sex, and rolled her hips to rub herself on him.

"And then do I say, yes, please, Evander?"

"No, lass," he sighed and touched his brow to hers. "That is when I wake up. I put my hand on my rod, and spill on my belly like a lad." He kissed her again, and then rolled away. "I shouldnae speak of it."

His complex emotions filled Rachel, who tried to sort them out. He despised himself for admitting that he came just dreaming about her, and for desiring her that much. He still felt betrayed by Fiona, and yet guilty that he wanted another woman. The old, hard feelings toward all women had gone, but he still distrusted her gender. More than anything he thought she was still damaged from what David had done, and that he might be seducing her into something she didn't want.

Rachel was stunned by his last thought, for it was the strongest of all. He hadn't acted on his desires because he was afraid of hurting her.

"You're right. You shouldn't talk about it. You should do it." Determined now, Rachel rose up onto her knees, and pulled the torn shirt over her head. "I'm not a dream, Evander. I'm right here, and I want you."

Evander climbed off the bed, and left the room before she could say another word. Rachel flopped back on the bed, feeling as if she might shriek her frustration, and then saw him return with a glowing lamp.

"I wish to see you," he said quietly.

He set the lamp beside the bed, and then took off his trousers, revealing the rest of his long, perfectly-muscled body. At first Rachel couldn't take her eyes off his swollen erection, but then she saw the faint scars gleaming all over his torso, arms and legs.

"What happened to you?" she whispered as she reached out to touch the widest, shiniest scar.

He glanced down at himself before he moved his shoulders.

"I have always been a warrior. 'Tis a hard life."

When he joined her on the bed she saw the primitive tattoo covering his chest take on a faint, dark blue glimmer, which distracted her from his scars.

"Your ink glows in the dark," she murmured as she gently traced the curve of one sphere.

"Do you think it unsightly?" he asked as he pulled her closer.

He was actually worried that she didn't care for it. To answer him she pressed her lips to the crossbar between the two circles.

Evander dragged her up and covered her mouth with his. He kissed her lips apart and stroked her tongue with his so hungrily that Rachel felt as if she were melting into him. His fingers tangled in her hair, and his arm clamped hard across her back. When he toppled over with her, his hands went everywhere as he wedged his hips between her legs.

He shifted her thighs up around him as he pressed his thick cockhead against her, parting her and penetrating her with a single jerk of his hips. She thought he might ram into her, but he stopped and gripped her hands, bringing them to his mouth to kiss her fingertips.

"You make me a lad again," he said as he braced himself on one elbow. Then he slid his other hand under her bottom, holding her still as he pushed in another inch. "Dinnae hold me out. Let me come into you."

"I want to." It had been so long since she'd had sex, however, that even with the slickness of her arousal she felt too tight to take him. "It's just that you're so big, and I'm…a wee wisp of a wench."

Evander's expression softened. "So you are, lass." He turned onto his side, and tugged her against him, lifting her leg to rest on his hip. He reached down to wedge his bulbous tip between her folds. "There, now. 'Tis no reason to hurry. We've the night. We can enjoy just this."

Rachel couldn't believe he was holding back for her. She could feel how much he needed to be inside her.

"Not for the whole night, I hope."

"We've naught else to do," he chided.

She trailed her fingers over his ink, and shifted closer until she could press her breasts against him. Feeling that thick wall of muscle on her tightly puckered nipples made her eyelids grow heavy.

"I like being naked with you."

"I'll burn our garments, and spend the winter here." He stroked her thigh, and shifted his hand to slide between them. "Would you like that?"

"Until we starve," Rachel murmured and closed her eyes for a moment as he parted her and found her clit. "Or we could move the pantry in here."

"The heart of your pearl beats for me," he said and lightly pressed his thumb against her, gently massaging the pulsing nub. "'Tis good when I pet it so?"

"Ah, 'tis great." Her voice sounded almost ragged as she rubbed back against the pad of his thumb. "But if you keep doing that, I'm going to come, and…I'd like to have you inside me when I do the first time."

"So you shall," he murmured.

Rachel caught her breath as he began to move, filling her by slow, gradual degrees. Although his shaft stretched her to the brink of pain, her pussy gloved him with wetness. He kissed her as he made one last, gentle thrust to bury himself inside her, and groaned as she tightened around him.

"'Tis better than any dream," he said against her lips.

The heat of his mouth and the slow rub of his thumb against her pearl added countless sensations to the intense feeling of being impaled by his long, hard shaft. Need blazed low in her belly like a spreading fever, and then what Evander felt poured into her. Rachel felt the silky clasp of her softness on him, how hard he'd clamped down on his desperate need to thrust into her, and the deep, pounding pulse in his tight balls.

The blend of their needs and pleasures rushed through her like dark light.

"Evander."

"Yes, my lass, my Rachel," he crooned. "All of it, all of you, mine now."

In the space of a heartbeat Rachel felt herself gush around him as a waterfall of bliss poured over her, her body gripping him even tighter as she gave herself over to it. She heard him make a guttural sound, and then he was riding it with her, his cock pumping into the heart of her delight.

The room spun. Rachel felt the linens beneath her shoulders and then Evander atop her, his big body working over and inside her. The bed posts drummed against the wall as he fucked her with long, powerful strokes, her pussy so wet now she could hear the sexy liquid sound of each penetration. Yet when she tried to caress his chest he gripped her wrists and pinned them to the bed.

"I'll no' last if you touch me now," he bit out, his jaw tight and the sinewy muscles in his arms bunching. "I'll feel your sweetness again before I spill. Give me what I want, Rachel."

"This?" she asked, and clenched around him

as he plowed into her, and felt the aching surge building at the base of his shaft. Her body responded with another cascade of silky, wet heat, and when he felt it Rachel cried out with delight. "Oh, yes."

"Aye." He watched her face as he plunged slowly in and out, stroking her climax until she finally shuddered through the last stream of it and went boneless beneath him. "Now for you. Have me, lass."

He wrapped his arms around her as he buried his cock in her pussy, clutching her against him as he grunted. Inside her his cock swelled, impossibly thick, and then jerked with the force of his ejaculation.

Rachel cried out with every spurt he pumped into her, feeling his masculine pleasure along with her own. He came with all the intensity of a missile, unwavering and powerful, and shook with satisfaction and relief as he flooded her throbbing pussy.

Tucking her hot face against his damp neck, Rachel sighed with utter contentment. When he released her wrists and tried to withdraw from her she shook her head.

"No, please. Stay inside me."

He looked down at her, and moved enough for her to feel his shaft, which hadn't gone completely soft.

"If I do, I'll have you again. 'Tis too much for you."

She hated to admit it, but he was probably right, and let him go.

"It's not because of my size. I haven't done this since I was in college." She might as well tell him the rest. "David and I never made love."

"Oh, so he's a blind, daft fool as well as a filthy back-stabbing arse of a coward, gods rot him." He propped his head on his hand and studied her face. "Why no'?"

"He said it would be romantic to wait until we were married. I believed him." She met his gaze. "I'm glad. If we had, I think I'd probably never feel clean again."

Evander looked uncertain, as if he wanted to tell her something.

"You and Fiona were lovers," she said.

"Before we came here, aye. After, Fiona didnae want me so much. Near the end, no' at all." His mouth flattened. "I didnae understand it, but I let her be."

Rachel caught a glimpse of a memory of

Evander's lover huddled on the bed and weeping, while he tried in vain to comfort her.

"That was kind of you."

"I couldnae relieve her terrors, nor remove her guilt. She lived in fear that we would be found." He moved onto his back and stared up at the ceiling. "Mayhap she should have left me. I killed her as much as the plague."

"You can't blame yourself for her illness," Rachel told him. "Besides, you took her away from everyone who would have hurt her." She crawled up onto his chest. "You protected her. You kept her alive."

"Now you are kind." He stroked his hand over her hair. "I had never been loved before Fiona. I used her for my pleasure and thought naught of it. Yet when she offered her heart, nothing more mattered to me but that. Now I wish I'd gone to the laird, and asked him to spare her. Had Lachlan been told of how ill she had been used, I think he would have."

"I should have listened to my father when he warned me about David. He never liked or trusted him, and he was a very good judge of character." She gave him a wan smile. "I'd never been in love before, though, and I was so sure that

David was my future. Every time I looked at him, I felt it."

Evander reached over to blow out the candle. "And what do you feel now?" he asked as he drew the tartan up over them.

Rachel cuddled closer. "I'm where I should be."

Chapter Eleven

FROST CRYSTALLIZED THE remains of the garden each morning, until one day when the temperature rose unexpectedly, and a storm rolled over the ridges to soak the highlands. Rachel covered the windows with oiled cloths Evander used to keep out the rain, while he hauled all of the water storage urns out into the deluge to fill them. She grinned as she carried out two empty buckets to add to his urns.

"This definitely beats hauling water from Splang or the river," she said and eyed the dark clouds billowing over them. "How long will it last?"

"Some hours," he said and caught her by the waist and dragged her up against him. "You're all wet, Mistress Ingram."

"I guess I am," Rachel said and linked her hands behind his neck. "Maybe you should take me inside and dry me off, Master Talorc."

Whenever she called him that his eyes darkened with sensual hunger, so it was no surprise when Evander lifted her off her feet and carried her into the cottage. Inside he set her down by the fireplace, and gave her a deep, hungry kiss as he unfastened and stripped off her sodden clothes. When she tried to do the same for him, he shook his head and reached for the shawl she'd left on his chair.

"'Twill be tonight for that, my wee wanton wench," Evander said as he wrapped her up and deposited her in the chair. "Rain brings the red grouse to shelter in the forest, and I mean to hunt them while they're yet young and sweet."

She pretended to glower. "You're leaving me here naked so you can chase little brown chickens?"

"Stay inside, and keep the hearth hot." He tucked her shawl up under her neck, and kissed her until she gasped against his mouth. "I'll fetch in the urns and buckets when I come back."

Rachel watched him collect his spears and heavy cloak, and sighed a little when he strode out into the rain. He was only going to hunt the game birds because he knew how much she liked them. Ever since they had become lovers he'd been pampering her that way. She'd caught a glimmer of worry from him, too. Last night he'd barely let her sleep. A lovely wave of sensation spread through her as she stretched her slightly sore body. As long as he kept making love to her like that, she'd be a very happy insomniac.

After she retreated to the bed chamber to put on a dry gown, Rachel went into the cold pantry to survey what she'd need for their evening meal. After she'd described a rotisserie to Evander, he'd chiseled a recess into the tops of two rectangular stones. Using an old spear with an iron shaft, he carved a wooden crank handle and fitted it to turn it into a spit to rest atop the stones. The medieval spit worked so well she didn't have to stew or braise game anymore.

She wanted to do something special with the red grouse, and thought of her father's favorite dish: roasted chicken stuffed with golden chanterelles. The last time she had walked through the clearing by Splang she'd noticed the exact same mushrooms growing on the roots of an old oak. With their apricot scent and peppery flavor, they'd make the perfect stuffing.

To get them, she'd have to go to the clearing by herself.

Therein lay the problem. Rachel knew why Evander didn't want her wandering around on her own. He'd thought about it every time they went gathering. As beautiful as the highlands were, they could also be very dangerous. Sometimes seemingly level ground sheared off and became a cliff with a deadly drop. Sheep, cow and deer herds roamed the slopes, and if spooked could attack or even stampede. She knew from living in SoCal that the rain might cause a flash flood to come out of nowhere. If she was smart, she'd stay in the cottage.

As Rachel brooded over the dilemma, she heard the rain slow to a light drizzle. She'd been to the clearing enough times to know where it was safe to walk. Picking the chanterelles wouldn't take long, and she knew Evander would appreciate them.

"I'll be careful," she muttered under her breath as she grabbed her cloak and a gathering basket.

Outside the air gave Rachel a wet smack in

the face, and she tugged the tartan up over her head as she hurried down the stone path and out through the gate. It wouldn't do for her to slip on the wet grass, fall and break something, so she forced herself to slow down. Somehow the clearing seemed farther away than she remembered, but whenever she went out with Evander she paid more attention to him than anything else.

Because I'm falling in love with him.

It wasn't just the stunning, wild, magical sex. Rachel loved how beautifully they suited each other, with Evander's aggressive masculinity meshing perfectly with her compliant feminine nature. In her time she'd often felt embarrassed by her desire to please, but with her highlander it felt completely natural. It also excited her deeply to be so wanted by a man that he would forget to be civilized around her.

Yet while she enjoyed every minute of their love making, her heart reacted just as passionately when Evander said her name or came near or just looked at her. Being alone with him, taking care of the cottage and sharing her days and nights with him had changed her. She would never have thought she'd be content with such a simple life, but it was pure and real. She still had so much to learn, but that made every day seem like an adventure.

She also knew Evander wasn't perfect. He struggled with his temper, and he carried around a war spirit that could be intimidating, and probably quite lethal. He was still keeping things from her, or thought he was. He'd had serious issues with women until he'd found love with Fiona, and that still worried her. He'd definitely made some terrible mistakes. All the hardship and betrayal and heartbreak he'd suffered should have ruined him.

But it hadn't.

Rachel knew who Evander was in his heart. She saw the man the rest of the world had never glimpsed. Life may have forged him into a weapon, but the cold, hard warrior was only a façade. Beneath it was a weary man who simply wanted to be loved.

Fack, but she's a ripe one. I'll swive her 'til the snows come, and then back to Agna and the bairns.

For the first time since Rachel had crossed over, the voice in her head didn't belong to Evander. She felt lust and gloating accompanying the words, and looked ahead to see a sizable herd of brown and ivory sheep grazing in the clearing.

She'd seen a few of them before in the distance, and had been charmed by their curved horns and dense, wooly coats, but they'd never come close to the cottage.

By season's end he'll marry me, a happy female voice said behind her eyes. *The master shall give us a cottage, and I can bring Mam to live with us.*

Carefully Rachel moved forward until she saw the man and woman taking shelter under the big oak above the clearing. They were embracing beneath the protection of a cloak spread over the lower branches. A shepherd's crook stood leaning against the tree, and a basket mounded with loose brown wool sat next to it. The man was unlacing the woman's blouse.

Rachel couldn't get to the chanterelles without passing within their view. She either had to brazen it out, or go back to the cottage empty-handed.

Taking a firmer grip on her basket, she walked down the last stretch of path to the fallen tree, which now lay covered by dozens of the golden mushrooms. As she picked the smallest of the chanterelles, the thoughts and feelings of the couple under the trees poured into her mind.

Coira, the young shepherdess, was happy her farmer master had sent Parnal, the drover, to help her roo his sheep, which involved plucking the loose wool from their coats. The messy task took a long time, so they could dally a little without raising suspicion. Parnal felt smug over how flattery and a few false promises had gotten him into Coira's arms.

Rachel tried to ignore their thoughts as she filled the basket, but then the drover began gloating over his immediate future plans. The shepherdess had no idea that once the sheep were brought in from the ridges to spend the winter at the farm, Parnal would be leaving to return to his wife and children, with no intention of returning.

She lifted her head to stare at the couple. The drover thought it funny that he'd duped the shepherdess into believing he'd marry her. He prided himself on how fertile he was, and fully expected to leave her pregnant. He didn't care that without a husband that would condemn her to an even harder life, trying to raise a child by herself. The worst thought came from Parnal as he began to hike up Coira's skirts.

Mayhap she'll die giving birth to the brat. 'Twould serve the little hoor proper.

Rachel stiffened. The drover had the same, smarmy tone to his thoughts as she'd heard in

David's voice when he'd said, *Please, just shut up and die.* She straightened, grabbed her basket, and marched up the slope until she stood a few feet from the couple.

On some level she knew she was making a mistake, but she didn't care. She was sick of men who thought the women they used should die horrible deaths. She'd never be able to get back at David for what he'd done, but she wouldn't let another woman be victimized.

"Excuse me."

Parnal shot up with a yelp, while Coira yanked down her skirts and bolted to her feet.

"What do ye here, ye nosy cunt?" the drover demanded, hurriedly fastening his pants. "We're busy now. Go on with ye."

"You should know that he's already married," Rachel told the shepherdess, and had to raise her voice to be heard over Parnal's subsequent blustering. "His wife's name is Agna, and she lives with their three children in the lowlands. He's only here to make enough money to start his own flock. You know, for Agna, and the kids." She regarded the gaping drover. "Also, he thinks you're a whore."

"How could ye ken what I am, what I think?" Parnal demanded.

Coira drew back her arm, and slapped the drover so hard it knocked him on his ass. After she grabbed her crook and her wool, she walked down to Rachel.

"How could ye ken?" she demanded. "Has he swivved ye, too?"

"I was married to someone like him," she told Coira. "Trust me, you're better off dumping his ass right now."

The shepherdess looked back at Parnal as if he were scum, nodded to Rachel, and stalked off.

Parnal scrambled to his feet. "Wait, lass, 'tis naught but lies. I'd never...*fack*." He turned on Rachel. "Who told ye about Agna? Elpin? Mathis?" His eyes narrowed. "They dinnae ken about Coira and me. None do."

"They will now." Judging by the ferocity of Coira's thoughts, Rachel suspected that everyone in Scotland would. "Maybe she'll get word to your wife. Or does Agna know how much of a whore you are? No? She thinks you're completely devoted to her and the bairns? I see. So you've duped her, too. Bravo."

"No wench could pluck the thoughts from my

head as ye do. Ye dinnae even speak like a Scot."
The drover drew a dagger, but backed away from
her as if she terrified him. "Ye're a witch."

"Don't be ridiculous." The blazing outrage
Rachel felt suddenly fizzled out in a wave of cold
fear. In this time women believed to be witches
were drowned or burned alive. "I'm from the
lowlands. I...I know your family."

"More lies. Ye're as much a lowland wench as
I'm the king." Parnal jabbed at the air between
them. "Begone with ye, witch, before I cut out yer
heart and feed it to the flock."

Since he looked scared enough to make good
on the threat, Rachel turned and hurried down to
the trail. The drover didn't follow her, but Rachel
didn't feel safe until she was back inside the
cottage, her shoulders pressed against the door
and her basket falling to the matting. Little
chanterelles bounced out to scatter around her
muddy boots as she pressed a hand to her cold,
wet face, and breathed deeply until her heart
stopped pounding so fast.

For the rest of the afternoon Rachel kept
checking the back windows, but the drover never
appeared. Nor did she pick up any more thoughts
from him or Coira. But now she felt pretty sure

that she could read someone's mind only when she was in close proximity. That didn't put her in the clear, and when Evander returned from his hunt she steeled herself to confess what she had done.

"Your wee brown chickens, my lady," he said, holding up a large string of the game birds to show her. "I'll clean them once I've carried in the urns, and we'll spit them." He spotted the gathering basket on the table. "Orachs, good. They'll make a fine stuffing."

"I thought so, too," she said faintly. "We, ah, call them chanterelles in my time."

"Sounds Francian," Evander said and bent his head to kiss her, his wet hair soaking her bodice. He straightened and his brows drew together. "We'd no orachs in the pantry. You went out gathering while I was hunting."

"I did, but only to the spring." All the breath rushed out of her. "Please don't be angry with me. I wanted to surprise you with the mushrooms. I didn't know you knew what they were."

"We're not complete savages, lass." He studied her face. "I ken that you want some freedom, but 'tis too dangerous. Promise me you willnae go alone again."

She knew that if she confessed to the confrontation with the drover, Evander would be furious, and not just with her. She'd also have to reveal her ability, and that wasn't something she wanted to tell him when he was angry.

Rachel nodded. "I won't. You have my word."

Chapter Twelve

"TRIBUNE SENECA," SAID a sentry. He slapped his forearm across his chest plate and bowed as Quintus emerged from his sleeping chamber. "The prefect left word for you."

Ermindale wouldn't entrust anything important to a sentry, but he might as well hear it.

"Tell me."

The sentry straightened. "The prefect expects the ship from Wick to arrive at midnight. He requests your attendance in the great hall for the reports."

"Very well," Quintus said and nodded before continuing down the passage.

Cargo ships sailing along the northern Scottish coastal routes had begun arriving a day or two late to port, but thus far no one suspected why. Quintus timed the legion's raids on the vessels so that they took place so far out at sea that no one witnessed the attacks. The ship's owners had no idea that their vessels had been first brought to Isle of Staffa, where the undead enthralled the crews. Using the mortal sailors as spies for the Ninth had been Ermindale's idea.

"They'll act as scouts, and gather information for us at every port of call," the marquess had said when he proposed the new enterprise. "Every harbor town trades in gossip as well as goods. We show every sailor the portrait card of the wench, so they will look for her."

Quintus had been surprised by how well the scheme had worked. The spy ships stopped at Staffa en route to their destinations, and their captains dutifully reported to Ermindale with what they had learned while in dock. Thanks to them they knew the McDonnels were also searching for Talorc and his woman. Ermindale had sent word to their mortal thralls in the villages and towns to misdirect the highlanders with false sightings. The undead had yet to find the pair, but with the McDonnels looking everywhere Talorc was not, they had the definite advantage.

Tonight Ermindale was expecting the *Raven* to arrive with another shipment of his turned slaves from the south, as well as one of the merchant ships, and would remain above ground to keep watch for them. That left Quintus to spend his evening more agreeably, first by examining the magnificent volumes brought back from a raid on an abbey, and then by attending to his less intellectual needs.

"See that I am not disturbed," he told the passage guards before entering the cave that served as his private library.

Ermindale had catered to Quintus's every whim when creating the library, transporting fine furnishings and carpets from one of his estates, and having the builders fashion sealed cabinets for the tribune's every-growing collection of illuminated manuscripts. He'd even managed to put in a hearth, with a flue to channel the smoke up through a natural vent in the stone. Quintus often spent hours sitting by the fire and staring into the flames as he contemplated their progress. The Isle of Staffa protected them, the turned slaves had swelled their depleted ranks, and their thralls would happily kill for them. He never indulged in idle satisfaction, but for the first time since the Ninth had been cursed Quintus saw a future for the legion.

The seven manuscripts taken from the abbey proved to be the most ornate Quintus had ever seen. As he carefully inspected them, he took great pleasure in reading Latin again, and admired the monk's intricate embellishments on the borders of the pages. Yet as much appreciation as they inspired, the accounts they contained represented the real treasure. He had been doggedly researching every resource he could find on the early pagan tribes of Scotland, in hopes of learning something that might explain the curse the McDonnels had used to change the legion into undead.

In this volume he found descriptions of several heathen rituals, which shared some connection with the strangely-carved stones the early tribes had left scattered all over Scotland.

On their Day of Choosing the young men of the tribe would be offered as living sacrifices to demonic spirits. The images of the demons would be inked onto their bodies, so better to possess them at their leisure. These marked warriors often proved to be formidable fighters, for they believed the spirits gave them unholy powers.

From the monk's rendering of the primitive tattoos in the page's borders, Quintus decided that the tribesmen had to be the same race as the McDonnel Clan. He frowned as he read the next passage.

Marked warriors had their choice of the most desirable young females, who when taken as wives were also demon-marked in smaller form. This ritual was never observed, as the warriors performed it in secret. The tribes believed that a demon-marked wife would do anything to protect her warrior—even sacrifice her own life.

If the account was true, then it was possible that the highlanders had their own form of enthrallment. Another of many similarities between the legion and the clan, it seemed. That they shared so many peculiarities that were not found in the mortal world intrigued him. If he could collect enough manuscripts on the subject, he might even ferret out why.

The door to his library opened and closed, and the scent of night-blooming flowers painted the air. Quintus closed the manuscript and rose from his desk before he faced his creation.

"I told you to wait in your chamber for me, my dear."

"I tire of waiting each night."

As white as the milk she had once carried in pails, Fenella stood wrapped in his scarlet battle cape, her icy blonde hair cascading in long, thick waves that curled around her hips. Her once pale-blue eyes now gleamed as black as his own, and the red flush on her lips told him she had fed only minutes ago.

"Why do you go to your books when you might come to me?" she asked. "They cannae give you pleasure. They only sit there and do naught."

"You require much more attention," he said. He went to her and bent to kiss her mouth, but she turned her face away. "Very well. We'll return to your chamber to discuss the matter."

"To lock me away again, you mean." She shrugged out of the cape as she rubbed up against him. "So that dried-up old one willnae see what you have done. I move too fast for any eyes to glimpse me, you ken that." She slid her cool hand up to his mouth, and rubbed her finger against the tips of his fangs. "I am your great secret, am I no'?"

Saving Fenella from death by changing her into an immortal had taken only a full day, as it did with the mortal males they turned, but it had also resulted in some unexpected oddities. The most startling, her ability to move with unearthly speed, was a talent which none of his men shared. Her sweet, willing nature had also been transformed into a dark, demanding seductiveness. She'd become as strong as any of his men, but the vicious cunning she displayed grew more dangerous each night. After she drained a half-dozen thralls by slashing their throats and bathing in their blood, Quintus had begun locking her in her bed chamber. But now it seemed not even that would contain her.

"You didnae come to me last night," Fenella said, pouting. "I was so lonely I facked a guard. His cock was like this." She pinched the air.

Quintus felt her dark, sweet scent growing stronger, as it always did with her lust. It stirred his own.

"Come," he said gripping her arm. "I will fuck you."

"No' now. Bring a lass for us to share later. I like to suck their teats while you fack them in the arse."

She easily pushed him away and picked up the cape, wrapping it around her again before she blurred and vanished. Quintus went after her, but as soon as he stepped out into the hall he paused. All of the guards had vanished, and then he saw the piles of dust edging the stone floor. His jaw set as he glanced at the hidden passage that led to her chamber. He didn't care how many mortals she killed, but murdering his men—her own kind— could not be tolerated.

He wondered with her speed if he could kill her by himself, and decided not to risk it.

"Tribune Seneca." Quintus turned to find the deceptively wizened-looking Ermindale as he came out of a passage. "Our sea-going spies have brought news of great interest from Wick. Will you join us?"

Hiding his impatience, Quintus accompanied the marquess to the great hall. There he listened as the merchant captain reported a story about a dark-haired witch who had bespelled a shep- herdess and attacked a drover in the northern highlands. Rife with the usual superstitious nonsense, the tale itself didn't interest him, but he had the captain repeat the drover's description of the witch.

"A petite woman with black hair and dark eyes who spoke strangely, my lord," the mortal said. "He didnae understand many of the words she uttered, but said that she used her unnatural powers to pluck the very thoughts from his head."

"If true, what a prize she would be, Tribune," Ermindale murmured.

"Indeed," Quintus agreed.

The other two druidesses who had joined the McDonnel Clan both had spoken strangely and used unfamiliar words. The first had used her fiery power to incinerate his predecessor. The second was a skilled tracker who had led the McDonnels directly to the legion's new stronghold on the mainland before they could complete it.

"Bring me the portrait card," Quintus ordered.

Ermindale retrieved the strange miniature, and Quintus read again all of the letters and numbers on it. Three groups of four numbers read 1994, 2012, and 2020. If they represented years, then the numbers before them might be months and days. The card itself looked far too perfect to be created by even the most skilled hand. Something about the oddity seemed just beyond his grasp.

"How did this witch appear in her person?" he asked the captain.

The mortal shrugged. "The drover remarked on how clean and comely she was, and how she had all her teeth still."

"I want the woman captured and delivered to me unharmed," Quintus said and handed the card back to his prefect. "We will sail to Wick, and have this drover lead our hunters into the highlands. They can bring her to the ship."

"What of Talorc?" Ermindale asked, frowning.

"If she has the power to read a mind, by now she knows the traitor's," Quintus said. "She will lead us to Dun Aran. Or we will hold her until Talorc comes for her, and use her to persuade him to reveal the location."

He ordered Ermindale to prepare for their sea journey, and then left the hall to attend to his murderous undead lover. He found Fenella sitting in her chamber, dressed properly and studying a large book.

"Fair evening, my lord." She tore a page out, crumpled it and tossed it into the fire. "You didnae bring me a pretty mortal."

Quintus eyed the book, and when he recognized it as one of his precious manuscripts he snatched it from her hands. A glance at the hearth made him shudder. It contained the scorched covers of the six others she had stolen from his library.

"How could you do this?" he demanded.

"'Tis no' trouble to destroy lovely things, my lord." In a blur of motion she grabbed the manuscript from his hands and threw it into the flames. "There. Now you've no reason to keep me waiting. Or shall I burn all the others you've hoarded away, to be sure?"

Quintus caught her before she could speed away and threw her across the chamber. Fenella laughed as she crashed into a trunk, making it explode into a burst of shattered wood and broken iron. She pushed herself upright, grinning as she brushed off her skirts.

"Why are you angry? You say I am your dear, your love, your precious beauty. If that is truth, nothing should matter to you but me." She tore at her bodice until her breasts spilled out of it. "Am I no' your sweet maiden still? Do you no' desire me? Do you no' want to fack me until I bleed from every hole?"

His rage abruptly dwindled. "Fenella, I would never hurt you."

"Oh, but you have, my grand lover. You took me from the dairy, and brought me to this privy of an island. You drank my blood, and bespelled me, and used me as your hoor. You might have let me die, but no. You made me into a blood-drinker." Her voice rose to a shriek. *"Why did you do this to me?"*

Quintus crouched down in front of her. "I could not let you die."

"And now you wish you had. I've felt it since you turned me. You look upon me as you would a serpent, ready to strike." She reached out to him, her small hand curling into his as the madness vanished from her eyes. "Here is what I ken. I cannae be your prisoner or your hoor, Tribune. I'm no' a thrall."

He'd underestimated her intelligence, which also seemed to be increasing by the day.

"Fenella, you could be so much more."

"Aye, and I am. I'm undead, same as you and the others." She pressed her cheek to his. "Make me legion, or end me."

He drew her to her feet, and cradled her face as he kissed her cold lips. Her beauty no longer tore at his heart, for now he finally saw her for what she was, what he had made her. He could no more take pleasure in her body than he could one of the men.

"I command the legion," he told her. "If you are to be one of us, then you must obey me in all things. No more slaughtering thralls, or killing guards, or destroying my precious things."

"As you say," Fenella said as her eyes narrowed. "What am I to do, then?"

Quintus smiled a little. "To begin, you will serve as my personal bodyguard. You will protect me with your life, and I will teach you how better to use your powers for me and the legion. Prove to me that I can trust you, and you will have much more."

"Pretty mortals?" she said, sounding almost amused.

He nodded. "There are thralls for pleasure, but you need not cut their throats to have it of them. Save your blade for the McDonnels."

Fenella's gaze shifted as the door to the chamber opened. Ermindale stepped inside. In a flash she had him pinned against a wall, her dagger poised over his heart.

"Dougal," Quintus said as he came over to

rest his hand on Fenella's shoulder. "Permit me to introduce our newest recruit, Optia Fenella."

"A pleasure," the marquess said as his eyes shifted down. "Mayhap persuade the optia to no' cut off my head? I've a message from the mainland that cannae wait."

"Release him," Quintus ordered. Once she had, he handed her the keys to his own chambers. "Move your things to my quarters. I will see you there after I speak with the prefect."

He walked with Ermindale into the corridor, where the marquess slammed the door shut and scowled at him.

"Are you out of your wits? You cannae turn wenches to serve us."

"I am tribune, and I can do as I please," Quintus informed him. "What is the message?"

"There isnae," the old man snapped. "I saw what that crazed cunt did to the guards outside your library, and I feared for you. I have turned a blind eye so you could have your pleasure of her, but this must end now."

A thought suddenly occurred to him. "Why?"

"Because you dinnae see what she is becoming," Ermindale said and stabbed a finger at

Fenella's door. "She's mad, like a foam-mouthed dog. I'll no' have her—"

"It was you who had her drained when she was a thrall," Quintus said, and saw the flicker of panic in the old man's eyes. "I thought as much. You did not care for my affection for her. Or did you mean to enslave her to you, so that she might act as your spy, like every other thrall in this stronghold?"

"I had to put an end to her," Ermindale said, baring his teeth. "You spent every moment you could between her legs. She was a weakness you couldnae afford, and now she's even more dangerous to your command."

"You are my second, Dougal, and I value your advice." The tribune leaned in. "But your interference with Fenella is reason enough for me to end your immortality. Meddle in my affairs again, and I will. Am I clear?"

"Perfectly, Tribune," the marquess said and stepped back. He bowed stiffly. "I only hope you dinnae end up gracing her blade." He stalked off.

Fenella slipped out of his chambers and came to stand beside Quintus.

"I listened at the door. I didnae ken he meant to have me killed. In truth I never saw who did it.

They came from behind me." Malice brightened
her black eyes as she looked up at him. "May I
have him for my pleasure, Tribune?"

"Not yet, my dear. He is still of some use to
us, particularly with controlling the thralls." He
smiled a little. "Once I turn the witch, we will
have no more need of the marquess."

Chapter Thirteen

E VANDER WAITED UNTIL he felt
certain Rachel would not wake before
he got up and tugged on his trews. Out
in the front room he added some logs to the fire,
and eyed the cot beside it. If he kept away from
her, his ink would cease burning, and the war
spirit inside him would slumber again. But if it
remained awake, he would be spending the
remainder of the night in the barn.

Wake her.

She is ours.

We will take her together.

Evander crouched down in front of the
flames, bowing his head as he fought back the
spirit's demands. He didn't understand why it had

come fully awake. He'd been angry earlier, when she'd confessed to going out to gather the orachs alone. But he'd also understood that she'd done so only so she might please him with a fine meal. He'd been managing his temper better of late, thanks to Rachel's calming presence. Now that they'd become lovers he no longer constantly wrestled with unfulfilled hungers. Rachel had given him everything he'd wanted and more.

He couldn't fathom why the spirit wanted her. It only ever stirred when he fought. Since the spirit craved battle, blood, and death, it had no use for females. Fiona had never aroused his spirit at all. Nor had any wench he had lain with in the past.

I cannae bring you to Rachel. How do I tell her that she arouses you, war spirit? That you wish to be inside her as much as I do? That only her complete surrender will appease you?

The spirit's response proved as arrogant and demanding as ever.

Give her to me.

Evander could never allow it to take him anywhere near Rachel when he was like this: poised between himself and a spirit so savage only death satisfied it. As fragile as she was he would snap her in two.

"Couldn't you sleep?"

He stood up and turned as Rachel came to him, with only his old tartan covering her lovely nakedness. In that moment he understood, perhaps for the very first time since his Choosing Day, just how dangerous he was.

"The fire wanted tending. Go back to bed, lass."

"You can keep me warm," she said and reached out to him, but frowned as he moved away. "What's wrong?"

Quickly he turned his back on her. "Naught to concern you. Leave me be, Rachel." He bit back a groan as the war spirit rose inside him, pouring into his skinwork. "Please, do as I say. Now."

"Why are you angry?" She came around him. "Oh, my god. What is it doing to you? Are you in pain?"

He caught her hand before she could touch his chest.

"The strongest and most skilled men of my tribe were offered to the war spirit on their Choosing Day. On mine, it took me. It lives inside me, sleeping until I need its strength and power in battle. Then it wakes." He pushed her hand away. "With a female from my tribe I could fack her with it, and she would ken what to do. You dinnae, and I willnae harm you. Please, go away from me before I do."

Rachel peered at the ink darting across his chest, and then up at his face.

"It doesn't want to hurt me, and neither do you. It wants to have sex with me? Can it do that?"

"No. You're druid kind, no' Pritani," he said, and shuddered as his ink extended out from his flesh, as if it meant to grab her. "Even if it could, if I would permit it, the war spirit isnae gentle, lass. If we take you…'tis too much for you to bear."

"But it's part of you," she said and gazed upon the moving bends of the spear as if she were fascinated instead of repelled. "This is why you've been sleeping in the barn? To hide this?"

He felt his self-control begin to slip. "I willnae let it have you."

She dropped the tartan, and pressed herself against him. "Then I will."

Evander howled, but the sound died away as

the spirit flooded into his throat, and spoke through him.

"So you come to me at last, little wren. I have wanted you since we took you from the circle and brought you to our bed. Do you fear me on your flesh? Or will you take my spear between your soft lips, and in your snug little sheath?"

Rachel's expression grew solemn. "If Evander wants that, then yes, I will."

She knelt down on the tartan before him, her head tilted back as she waited.

"Dinnae resist us."

Evander's hands shook as he unfastened his trews, and watched as the inked spear straightened and slid down his belly to etch itself on his painfully erect cock.

Talorc wives knew how to submit when the war spirit made carnal demands, but Rachel had no experience or training. Yet when he brought his straining cockhead to her lips, she opened for him and took him into her mouth without hesitation. That she did so with the grace of a wife eager to soothe made him swell with new lust.

The simmering fury of the war spirit eased as she tugged on him, the velvet of her tongue stroking his shaft as she sucked. Evander gave her more, winding her hair in his fingers to guide her head as he facked in and out of her caressing lips. She made him feel like a god-ridden warrior of the ancient days, standing tall amidst the stones as the tribe's maidens were brought to be chosen as wives. Among the Talorc small, dark women like Rachel were rare, and treasured for their delicate beauty. Had he chosen her, he would have had to fight every unmarried man in the tribe to win her.

And then, for as many nights and days as the spirit rode him, he would bind her to his bed and pleasure her with mouth and hands and cock. Evander drew himself from her lips, and hauled her up against him, kissing the soft heat of her mouth.

"Will you give me all, lass? Can you?"

The moment she murmured yes he dragged her down to the floor, positioning her on all fours as he knelt behind her. Fisting his shaft, he rubbed himself from the ruck between her buttocks to the satiny pearl of her pleasure, and back to the slick opening now flowering for his first thrust.

"Please, please," she begged him. "I need you."

Crouching over her, he parted her and entered her, hissing in a breath as her honey melted around him. His hands curved over her jutting tits, squeezing them as he sank into her narrow quim.

The war spirit streamed into his cock and penetrated her with the spear of ink, and Rachel cried out as Evander began to stroke in and out, plundering her with his rod as his spirit sheathed itself in her.

"Now you feel us both, lass," he muttered against her ear, his hips slapping against her tight little arse as he facked deeper and harder. "We make you ours tonight, ours to have whenever we wish, on your knees and your back and your belly. You will give yourself to us as you do now, and we will take all your desires and make them ours. 'Tis no' so?"

"Yes," Rachel said, her body shaking with the force of his thrusts. Her quim fluttered helplessly as he impaled her and the spirit worked its hungry heat within her. "Oh, Evander, what is that?"

He reared back, bringing her with him and pushing her down on his cock as he gripped her breasts and pinched her nipples.

"Be still," he told her when she tried to move on him. "Close your eyes, aye, so that all you ken is us."

He clamped his hand under her jaw, seeking and finding the pulse of her heart. He stroked the beating vein as the spirit moved up through her, spilling heat everywhere it travelled, until it surfaced on her breast and flowed up her throat to leap back to his flesh.

Evander immersed himself in the spirit and her, and released the fury he had kept leashed for more than a year. If he had been in battle, he would have used his spear to pierce the heart of any enemy fool enough to come near him. Inside Rachel he grew even harder as he wrapped an arm around her waist, and drove his hips up. Facking her tight quim with the spear of his cock, and piercing her softness as deeply as he could, he reveled in her flesh. Beneath his hand he felt the low sounds she made as she took each hammering stroke, her shoulders trembling and her hips jerking.

"You are my mate. No man put hands on you again," he told her, the words laced with the ferocity of his spirit. "You surrender only to me. Say it."

A whimper stuttered from her, high and sweet, before she gasped out, "No one but you."

Evander pressed his inked hand over her left

breast, and felt the spirit jab itself there, marking her as his mate. She cried out as it brought her to bliss, and he held himself in her gripping tightness, shuddering with the force of his jetting cock as he spurted against the ring of her womb.

Rising with her still impaled on him, Evander carried her back into the bed chamber and lay with her atop the cold linens. He never wanted to be parted from her again, but he had to know if he had frightened her as much as pleasured her. Slowly he withdrew and gently turned her to face him, and felt startled when he saw her flushed, glowing face.

"You are *never* sleeping in the barn again," she told him, and shifted until her breasts nestled against the vault of his chest. "Unless you and the horses make some room for me."

Even in the darkness he could see the small, dark spear inked over her heart, and traced it with his fingertip.

"You bear my mark now, Rachel."

She tucked in her chin to study the skinwork.

"It's a miniature of yours," she said and took his hand and pressed his palm over her breast. "How did you do this?"

"The spirit chose you as my mate, and used

my skinwork to mark yours. 'Tis no' happened since I left my tribe." The memory of being cast aside by his betrothed no longer stirred Evander to anger, but after Rachel's unreserved, desirous surrender he wondered if anything would. "Does it trouble you?"

"I'll think of you every time I take off my clothes." Her eyelids drifted down. "Unless you make good on your threat to burn them."

Evander felt bemused by how accepting she was of what should have been a terrifying experience. She had given herself to him without reservation, as if she knew exactly what he meant to do, and how she should respond. A Pritani wife could not have been more loving. Yet Rachel had claimed to love her husband—so much so that she'd ignored her father's warnings—and spoke of seeing her future with him.

No, that wasn't right, Evander thought. She'd said she'd felt her future when she looked at her husband. But how did one feel such a thing?

A whispering sound came from her, and he glanced down to see that she'd fallen asleep in his arms. In that moment he could see her slumbering beside him for a thousand nights to come, and a deep pang of regret tore at his heart. Aye,

Rachel would be his, and mayhap in time come to love him, but nothing could change the fact that she was mortal. One day she would die in his arms, just as Fiona had, and he would spend the rest of eternity alone.

Chapter Fourteen

✣✣✣

EARLY THE NEXT morning Evander left Rachel sleeping and saddled the roan, riding to the river to plunge into the icy water. Bonding with the streaming, bubbling currents, he rode them to a small loch on the western edge of the highlands. Once he guided his mount onto the shore, he followed it to an impassible cliff, and there tethered the horse to a nearby tree.

The surface of the loch reflected the pale, cloudless sky and framed it with diamonds of silvery sunlight. Evander suspected these warm, gossamer days of the fall would end before the next full moon. Even now his breath whitened the chilly air, and night frosts had stripped all but the evergreens of their leaves. He could almost feel the sun growing more distant, and the creatures of the forests and mountains preparing their winter nests and burrows. So he would also have to do with his heart.

The decision had been easier than he'd imagined.

Last night he had held his lover and watched her sleep, and imagined how the years would pass for them. As a wanted traitor he would always have to remain in hiding. Rachel would not have children with him, but neither would she have family or friends. He would be her world, and perhaps that would be enough for her, but if he were captured and killed, she would have no one.

He wanted to give her more, to give every-thing, but he had nothing left. She needed the life David had stolen from her. Keeping her with him, Evander knew, was almost as bad.

But he had to be careful not to alarm her. Rachel might not wake before he returned to the cottage, but if she did he would tell her that he had been exercising the roan. After their morning meal he would present her with the saddle he'd made for her, and ride down to the village. On his last trip for supplies he learned there would be a fair today to celebrate the harvest, and he knew she would enjoy that. Their outing would be a happy one, and when they returned to the cottage he would make love to her for the rest of the night.

Their last day together should be joyous.

Feeling unseen, watching eyes, Evander removed his spear and daggers, placing them on the ground in plain view before he approached the brush at the edge of the cliff. If he had still been a clansman he would have strode through the illusion, but he'd lost that privilege when he'd betrayed the McDonnels. He stood beside the nearest stone with his arms slightly out, showing his empty hands.

Nearly an hour passed before a young lass in a short woolen robe emerged from the cliff. Her round face filled with innocent curiosity, but her ancient eyes remained wary. She inspected him openly.

"What do you want, Renegade?"

"I come to parlay for Rachel Ingram, who is druid kind."

Moving slowly, he took out the snip of hair he had stolen from Rachel while she slept, and placed it on the standing stone before backing away from it.

The druidess watched him as she retrieved the lock, and disappeared back into the cliff.

He knew approaching any druid settlement would be dangerous, but for his lady he'd had to risk it. As much as he wanted to keep Rachel with him, he knew she needed more than a hard life with a ruined traitor. In her time she had wealth and position, and if she chose to return to it, the druids could help her seek justice for what David Carver had done. If she remained unwilling to leave Scotland, then she should be with the clan who could properly protect her. He imagined Rachel and Kinley would become fast friends.

That prospect should have angered him. He had never cared for the laird's woman. But now he saw the man he had been as mostly blind. Rachel had helped him to see so many things in a better light.

The clan would help her settle into a new life. Evander didn't want to think of her with another man, but that, too, would likely come to pass. He wanted her to be happy, and to live a full, rich life. She could find a mortal husband who could give her children. She would make a wonderful mother.

The young druidess appeared again, this time

accompanied by two hooded ovates holding sharp-looking scythes. She held out the lock of hair.

"Where is she?"

Evander kept his expression impassive. "Safe."

"In your company? I think no'." She caressed the lock. "You wish to trade Rachel, like a cow?"

He eyed the men, who seemed to be poised to attack him. While he didn't feel greatly threatened —druids knew as much about battle as Evander did about casting spells—one of them might make a fortunate blow and cut off his head. Rachel had learned much, but she could not survive the winter alone. She might also take it into her head to go looking for him.

"I want naught," he told her. "'Tis for the lady's sake I come to parlay. Rachel cannae remain with me. I'm—"

"We ken what you are," the druidess said. "Do you ken what she is?" When he said nothing she made an impatient gesture. "Go and bring her to us."

He shook his head. "Send for Ovate Cailean Lusk. I will return tomorrow with Rachel. You will see to it that he takes her to Dun Aran at once."

"Shall we now," the lass said, glowering. "Mayhap you mistake us. We druids dinnae take orders from turncoats."

"Then I cannae give her to you. Forgive my intrusion."

As he kept an eye on the ovates, he carefully restored his weapons to their rightful places. He nodded to the lass, turned on his heel, and headed for his mount.

"Wait." When he swung around, the druidess said, "Why did you take the reader from the grove?"

That she knew how they had met, and the word she'd called Rachel made his ire rise, and his skinwork wake. He'd suspected his lover had some sort of seer ability, and now wondered just what she could read.

"An undead patrol caught scent of her blood. To leave her would have been to kill her." Evander gave her a thin smile. "Or worse."

"Odd. You are said to have little affection for females, and yet you rescue this one, of whom you ken naught." When he didn't respond to that, she said, "Mayhap you would have us believe you hold with your clan to protect druid kind. This would be the clan you betrayed."

He shrugged. "Believe what you wish. I mean only to see Rachel secure and away."

"But what of yourself?" the druidess persisted. "How do you ken that we willnae summon the McDonnels to wait on your return?"

Evander's temper finally boiled over. He marched up to the lass, ignoring the scythes brandished by her escorts.

"You desire my blood spilled upon your shores? Summon them. I deserve death for what I've done. Only be sure to remove the lady before I am ended. She has suffered enough horrors in her time and ours."

The lass made a rude sound. "Such a tender heart, for such a bad man."

"You would punish her far more than me," he countered. "What does that make you?"

"Interested." She exchanged a meaningful look with the two men, who lowered their weapons. "Very well, Renegade. We shall summon Ovate Lusk to attend you and the lady on the morrow. No other shall be invited, and no blood shall be spilt. You've my word on it. Now I'll have yours."

"I promise the same," Evander said and felt

torn between tremendous relief and crushing despair as he bowed. "My thanks, Mistress."

"I want naught from you," the lass said and smiled sweetly. "Only ken that if you break your word to me, I'll stuff those spears up your arse."

Chapter Fifteen

✦✦✦

THE RICH SMELL of morning brew woke Rachel, who opened her eyes to see Evander pulling on a pair of trousers. For a moment she admired the long, handsome stretch of his back, and then noticed his hair was damp. She glanced over at the sodden pile of clothes on the floor, which were creating a little puddle of their own.

"Is it raining again?"

His shoulders stiffened for a moment before he turned around and came to sit on the bed. "I had a swim."

"Oh. Then you're a crazy man, because the water is like ice now." She pulled him down for a kiss, and felt the heat radiating from his tattoo. "What's wrong?"

"Naught I can fix." He hauled her onto his lap and wrapped an arm around her, pressing her cheek against his shoulder. "There's a fair down in the village. They have dancing and games and all manner of food. I thought we'd spend the day there."

Rachel didn't care about a fair. She wanted to know what had him so upset that his ink was practically sizzling. Yet when she reached into his mind, all she saw was her own face, like a reflection. He wasn't thinking about anything but her.

"Maybe we should stay in today." She straddled his thighs, and pushed on his chest until he lay back. "We can dance and have food and play my favorite game, right here."

Evander tucked his arm under his head. "You've a favorite game?"

"Yes. It's called Loving Evander Talorc." She bent down, curtaining his face with her hair as she brushed her lips over the hard line of his mouth. She kissed his chin and the angular line of his jaw, and then worked her way over to his ear. "Do you want to know the rules?"

He ran his hand down the length of her spine. "Aye."

"There aren't any," she whispered, and nipped his earlobe.

Rachel rubbed her hands over his chest and shoulders as she left a line of soft, damp kisses stretching from his ear to his collar bone. She had to shift a little lower to lave her tongue over his flat nipples, which puckered and hardened in response. She could feel his erection hardening against the top of her belly, and sucked on one nipple until his penis had swollen so hard and thick she could feel it throbbing through his trousers.

His tattoo burned against her lips, but as she swept her tongue over his crossbar spear the heat changed. What had been feverishly hot now pulsed with delicious warmth, which she caressed with her lips and fingers.

"Oh," she groaned as she felt an answering heat spread over her left breast, and brought his hand to her mark. "Do you feel that? I think someone's waking up."

He rubbed his thumb over her ink. "It hardly sleeps since we mated."

"So that's why I always want you to touch my breasts. My ink is flirting with yours." She smiled as she moved his hand over her, nudging his palm with her hard nipple before she shifted lower. "Your spirit is driving me crazy, you know."

His brows arched. "How so?"

"It puts ideas in my head."

She pushed her hands under his hips to unfasten the laces at the back of his trousers, and then tugged them down to free his erect penis. She crawled backward off the bed to finish stripping him before she pulled off her night shirt.

When she went around to the opposite side of the bed, Evander looked up at her with a frown.

"I think you want the other end of me, lass."

"Be patient," she said and climbed up over him, straddling his shoulders and tucking her legs under his arms as she positioned herself. When she lay down on top of him she heard him make a rough sound as she presented her slick sex to his face. "I think you'll like this."

Rachel curled her fingers around his shaft, squeezing him gently as she whispered a kiss over his engorged cockhead. As she parted her lips to draw him in she felt his fingers stroke her folds apart, and then the heat of his breath just before he began licking her. Her breasts throbbed in response to the intimate kiss, and she rubbed

them against his belly as she slid her mouth down
and sucked on his cock.

The thrilling, sexy feel of Evander lapping at
her fueled Rachel's desire to give him the same
pleasure, and she began working her lips down on
his shaft with gentle, tugging strokes of her
mouth. His shaft jerked as she increased the pull
and lashed him with her tongue, and then she
worked the base of him with her fist, squeezing
and releasing with the rhythm of her sucking.
When she felt his thoughts pour into her she
focused on what aroused him the most, and then
caught a fleeting desire for her touch on the
tightly constricted bulge of his balls.

Rachel cradled his sack in her hand, and
caressed the softly furred flesh with her fingertips.
At the same time she went down on him as far as
she could manage, sealing her lips around him as
she held his cock in her mouth and sucked hard.
Evander made a deep sound that vibrated
through her pussy, and then worked two fingers
into her tight, wet opening as he tugged on her
clit, sucking it.

Under her fingers she felt the surge of his
semen, and felt the rigid swelling of his shaft that
preceded him coming. She pressed her pussy back

against his mouth as she stroked his penis with her fist, sucking at him until the first jet surged over her tongue. The taste of him pushed her from aching, tight need into a storm of sweet, sultry ecstasy.

More primitive thoughts filled Rachel's mind as she came, and spread through her as she drank Evander's silky come. It seemed half-memory, half-fantasy. She saw herself kneeling naked before him in a meadow filled with warriors holding torches, and strangely-carved stones in a circle. Someone had bound her wrists behind her, but she wasn't afraid. There she sucked his cock in front of the tribe, his tribe, while they watched. Some of the men caressed the bulges at their crotches, while others openly took out and stroked their own erections. But oddly it didn't seem obscene to her. She could feel their emotions, and they were honest and sensual.

This was his tribe, his ritual, his mating bond. He had chosen her as if she were a woman of the Pritani. His spirit had marked her. They were not simply connected now, they were joined.

The thoughts faded as they shuddered with the force of their climaxes, and when it was over Evander righted her and held her against his side.

"I *do* like that," he told her, making her laugh. "'Tis how such pleasures are shared in your time?"

"Yes, but I've never tried it before now," Rachel admitted. "I did read up on it, and I... practiced a couple times with a banana." She sighed. "I was going to have my first time on my wedding night."

"Hmmm. I am glad you didnae waste that on your spineless bawbag of a husband." Evander stroked his thumb over her tingling lips. "What is a banana?"

"A long, yellow fruit that's the right size and shape for practicing." She glanced down at his hand, which was shifting her legs apart. "And what are you doing down there, Master Talorc?"

"Playing your game," Evander said and ran his hand from her knee to the inside of her thigh, where he stroked her slick folds with his fingertips. "Open your legs to me. Aye, and wider." When she had parted her thighs he penetrated her with one long finger, pumping it gently in and out of her pussy. "You want me inside your quim still."

"I want that every second I'm awake."

She had never felt him more focused on her,

as if no one and nothing else in the world existed for him.

He studied her face. "'Tis the same for you, then, the need to be joined."

"Aren't we already?" she asked, shifting closer until her mark touched his. "Isn't that what this is?"

Evander dragged in a ragged breath. "I've taken you, and I've marked you. 'Tis enough now."

He didn't seem to be talking to her. "I want it all, my love."

Burning shadows welled into his eyes, and he groaned and shook as his ink began to dart down his abdomen and then the crossbar fell onto her belly and began inching up her body. Rachel's eyes went wide as she felt the ink, hard and hot, but knew not to resist it. It crawled between her breasts, spreading over them and then tightening as if the tattoo were fondling her.

"Evander, oh, god," she breathed, thrusting her mounds up into the strange, intensely arousing sensation.

The ink scrolled from her breasts to her throat, where she felt it split and race along her arms, dragging them up over her head. She could feel the pieces of tattoo rejoining at her wrists, effectively binding them together.

"Our willing captive," Evander said, his voice taking on a harder edge. "Bound to us and marked as our mate. What shall you offer for our pleasure?"

Rachel discovered she could still move her arms, and lifted her wrists over his head, settling them against his neck.

"Everything," she breathed. "All of me. Take what you want."

He pressed her knees up as he moved between them, his chest heaving as he rooted against her. His eyes remained locked with hers while he worked his cockhead into the ellipse of her opening. The tattoo tightened around her wrists as he gripped her bottom, and with a single, powerful thrust buried his cock inside her.

Rachel clutched at him as she absorbed the shock of the penetration, grateful that her earlier climax and his mouth had made her so wet. He had filled her so completely she could feel every inch of him, hot and hard inside her pussy, and that alone was going to make her come again.

Some of the blazing darkness left his eyes. "You called me your love."

"That's because I'm in love with you," she said. She hadn't meant to blurt it out like that, but he was so deep inside her that she couldn't think of something cleverer to say. "I know it's too soon, but let me love you anyway. You'll like—"

Evander cut her off by kissing her, his mouth almost desperate as he pushed in his tongue to stroke hers. His body shuddered over hers, and then he drew out of her, and plowed back inside, over and over, but he never stopped kissing her. He swallowed her gasps and cries and the shaking moan she uttered as she came on his pistoning cock. He fucked her through the wild delight and kept shafting her, their skins growing slippery with sweat. Rachel felt now what he had been thinking, as if nothing else existed but the two of them. Her world became his body over her, the bed rocking under them, the devouring hunger of his mouth, and the endless pumping of his swollen, satiny penis into the clenching, quivering suppleness of her pussy.

After an eternity Evander wrenched his mouth from hers, and brought his hand up to cradle her cheek.

"We are joined now. I am yours, Rachel."

He meant it, she realized as his feelings

flooded into her. He belonged to her, now and forever. His heart, his body, his soul. He was giving her everything he was, everything he would ever be. He would never touch another woman again.

Rachel finally understood the meaning of the ritual she had seen in her head. The men of his tribe demanded complete surrender from their mates, because once they had it, they gave the same to them. Then all of his memories poured into her, and she saw all at once the twelve hundred years that Evander had lived since his days with the Talorc tribe.

He hadn't been fantasizing about being an immortal warrior.

Her vision grayed as her whole body flushed, and she fell into a roiling sea of primal sensation. She had no name for what came next, only that it filled her head with soundless light, and wordless joy. She felt on fire from within and without, and at the same time submerged in the coolest, softest water. She could hear the high, helpless sounds she made, and the deep, harsh grunts from Evander as he poured into her, and they blended together into a symphony of pleasure.

For a long time Rachel lay holding him,

heaving in the air she'd forgotten to breathe and feeling him do the same. After what they'd shared she couldn't go on keeping the truth about her ability from him.

"I have to tell you something."

"Aye, and so must I you." His weight lifted, and he moved to her side, turning her to face him. In his mind he was remembering a beautiful lake surrounded by dark mountains. "Tonight, after the fair."

She didn't understand why he was so determined to take her to it, but if it would make him happy, she planned on doing that every day for the rest of her life.

"Whatever you want."

Chapter Sixteen

❧❦❧

KINLEY MCDONNEL LEANED over her sleeping husband and nuzzled the serpent inked across his chest. The skinwork responded to her with a lazy ripple of its lines, and a flicker of its forked tongue against her fingers.

"Brash wench, to wake your laird from the only good sleep he's had in days," Lachlan grumbled. "Why did you no' do it sooner?"

"I was thinking." She climbed atop him, her slender, naked body soaking up the warmth of his body heat. "Not about this." She shifted to cradle his morning erection between her thighs. "I want to go and visit Lady Gordon, and see the baby."

"Aye, that can be arranged." His big hands

splayed over her bottom. "She enjoys your company, but that isnae why you wish to go."

"I heard an interesting rumor," Kinley said. She rose up on her knees, teasing the engorged head of his cock with the slick seam it wanted to delve into. "Laird Gordon is often seen riding at night around his woods and tenant farms."

Lachlan's brows arched. "I ride at night. In fact, you ride at night. What of it?"

"He doesn't ride alone." She let herself sink down just enough to lodge the curve of his dome inside her opening. "He always takes his bodyguard with him. Just the bodyguard, no one else."

Lachlan's jaw tightened. "He's a laird, and one of the king's men, and no' a fool."

"Or he's up to no good somehow, and has the bodyguard, well, stand guard." She wriggled as he tried to urge her down on him. "Stop being so impatient for sex. We're having a conversation here."

"You're talking." He flipped her onto her back and plowed into her. "I'm facking you."

Kinley shivered as he began thrusting deep and hard, his thick cock filling and emptying her, and then his mouth came down on hers and she forgot everything but him. He pinned her down and worked inside until she came twice, and then shuddered and jerked as he pumped her full of his cream. When he fell beside her she curled up against him, and stroked the sweat-sheened vault of his chest.

"Gordon does naught wrong on his night rides," Lachlan finally said. "I cannae say more than that, but I am sure of it."

"Okay," she said simply and climbed out of bed. She went to wash, and then pulled on a gown so Meg wouldn't give her any grief. When her husband came up behind her and wrapped his arms around her waist, she stiffened. "Hey, sorry. You cannae say more, I cannae go for round two."

Lachlan sighed. "Gordon is an ally, and a private man. I have few secrets that I keep from you, but this 'tis one." He turned her face to him. "Tell me your suspicions, and I will dispense with them."

"Lady Gordon has asked for Cailean Lusk to visit her, about a dozen times, and yet he never shows." She draped her damp linen towel around his neck. "She thinks he's avoiding her, and it has something to do with Gordon. Then I heard Raen mention how often he sees the laird riding at night." She let out a breath. "Do we need to be worried about him? Could he be an undead thrall or something?"

Her husband smiled fondly. "No, love. Of that I can assure you. Since Cailean helped arrange the Gordon's marriage, I doubt he is dodging the lady. Perhaps 'twas some simple misunderstanding, or he is much occupied with other duties."

"He spent two days here last week playing checkers with Neac. Meanwhile, Lady Gordon is birding me about him like every other day." Kinley reached into the cabinet and showed him the sheaf of messages she'd received from Lady Gordon. "What do I say to her?"

Lachlan kissed the tip of her nose. "Give her messages on to Cailean. 'Tis his doing, so should be his remedy."

"So I'm his answering service now?" she said and nipped his chin. "All right, it's a good idea. You may have sex with me again."

He gave her his laird look. "I may have you whenever I wish."

"Prove it," Kinley said and then shrieked with laughter as he scooped her up and tossed her onto their bed. "Now that's more like it."

Chapter Seventeen

✦

AS SHE AND Evander rode along the narrow mountain path leading down to the village, Rachel silently blessed her father for insisting she take riding lessons. The medieval saddle her lover had made her turned out to be oddly comfortable, which given the heightened sensitivity between her legs was a blessing. Even minus the stirrups she'd used in her time, the tack fit her and the horse like a glove. The dappled gray, however, hadn't been ridden in weeks. Guiding the skittish mount down the unfamiliar, somewhat overgrown trail kept Rachel fully occupied until they entered a seaside glen at the base of the mountains.

She gave the horse a grateful pat. "We made

it, ah…" She looked at Evander. "What's her name?"

"The nag? She doesnae have one." He reined in the roan to stop beside her, and saw her expression. "Dinnae give me that look. Fiona and I had been running from the clan when I bought her. 'Twas enough for me that she was strong and sturdy."

She loved that he was beginning to talk about Fiona more openly.

"Well, I'm not going to call her 'the nag.'" She leaned forward to say to the horse, "How about Dancer?"

The mare ignored her and began cropping grass.

"You're not helping, Dancer," Rachel said, and then regarded Evander's horse. "Let me guess. He doesn't have a name either. Since he can swim underwater, let's call him Diver."

The grin vanished from Evander's face. "You cannae tell anyone of that, lass."

His body turning transparent flashed through his mind, as did the feel of bubbling currents and streaming through a river on the roan, with Rachel plastered against his chest. What she would have dismissed yesterday as another strange fantasy now became very real. Along with being an immortal, he was able to bond with water, and use it to travel long distances in just a few seconds.

Why had he been afraid to tell her about it? After all the magical, wild sex they'd been having with his war spirit and the tattoos, why would it worry him? And why was he now thinking about a lake beside a sheer cliff?

"I won't say anything," she said and frowned. "I think I can fake a passable Scottish accent, but what should I call you while we're in the village?"

He leaned over to kiss her. "I like 'my love.'"

As they rode across the glen Rachel was able to get a better view of the village, which was as small as Evander had said. Houses and cottages had been built along either side of a wide coastal road, with a center cluster of smaller structures that must have served as shops and storage buildings. She saw pens of pigs and goats, and a few crudely-fenced pastures dotted with cows and sheep.

To the east of the village dozens of tents and stalls occupied a large open area. Groups of people milled around jugglers, musicians and other performers. On one end wagons piled high with grain sacks, vegetables and fruits surrounded

a long table of farmers taking coins in exchange
for their crops. Dozens of children ran around the
tents, chased by barking dogs and a few harassed-
looking women.

When they reached the fair, some older boys
hurried over, and Evander dismounted, giving
them each a coin before he helped Rachel down.
She watched the pair lead their horses into a
pasture beside the tents, where another dozen
mounts were grazing. The boys released the
horses and climbed up on a stack of hay bales to
keep watch over the entire herd.

"Can those two kids really keep someone from
stealing the horses?" Rachel asked. "I mean, what
are they, twelve?"

"No one shall try to steal them," he told her as
he took her hand, and laced his fingers through
hers. "The villagers are honest, and outsiders ken
'tis no' wise to take anything from these people.
The blood of Viking raiders runs in their veins.
Their punishments were so brutal that the
Romans they captured would kill themselves at
the first chance."

"Okay," Rachel said and concealed a shudder
as she smiled up at him. "I mean, aye, my love. I'll
no' anger the village folk."

"Spoken like a wise highland lass," he said and kissed her brow. "I'll look in on the boys later."

They walked from the horse pasture into the center of the fair, where the delicious smells of roasted meat, spiced fruits and tangy ales engulfed them. Rosy-cheeked women tended the food cooking on stone-ringed fires behind the stalls, while their smiling daughters served it on sticks or plates fashioned from birch bark. In between the food stalls stood smaller carts piled with cloth-wrapped cheeses, wine jugs and sacked nuts. Rachel inhaled the wonderful scents, which made her empty stomach rumble.

"Did I mention that I'm starving?"

"Famished," he corrected sternly. "You need much feeding for such a wee wisp of a wench. Very well, what will you have?"

She glanced around them. "Would one of everything be too much to ask?"

Evander chuckled. "You'll no' be a wisp on the morrow."

He helped her choose from the fair's bounty, selecting the best of the cheeses, breads, sausages and spiced pears, as well as a jug of sweet cider. The villagers had set up tables and benches in one of the larger tents, where they sat down to eat. Rachel noticed a few curious glances, but no one stared outright. Yet she felt as if someone was.

"Dinnae look so uneasy," he said as he uncorked the cider jug. "I come to the village every few weeks. The people have grown accustomed to me."

Rachel nodded, but she couldn't shake the sense of being watched.

Evander took pleasure in feeding her bites of the food, until she borrowed his dagger and showed him how to make a sandwich. Once they had finished and returned the empty jug to the orcharder's stall, they walked over to listen to a red-haired woman with a handheld harp. She had a low, almost husky voice and, as she sang, Rachel tucked herself against Evander's side.

"In a wee cottage, she's waiting for thee
    where the highlands come down and kiss the sea
    and the heather blooms sweet and wild and free
    there you shall find your bonnie beauty.
    She dreams of thee as she watches the bay

and plucks at the harp that you gave her
to play

in her heart is the hope born again every day

that you'll come back to her safe from away."

"I'm GOING to cry if I keep listening to this,"
Rachel said and felt a tug on her skirt. She looked
down into a small, grinning face. "Well, hello
there."

"Fair day to ye, Mistress," the tow-headed
little boy said, showing her the gap in his baby
teeth. "Will ye come to play the thimble game?"

She glanced at Evander, who nodded, and let
the child lead her over to a white-bearded man
sitting behind a rickety crate. On the box were
three rusty-looking thimbles, and a small nugget
of what appeared to be gold.

"Find the gold, and 'tis yers," the elderly man
rasped as he placed the nugget under the center
thimble.

Evander handed him a coin. "You'll no'
pocket it."

"I dinnae run a thimblerig," the old man
snapped as he began moving the thimbles around,
switching their places so fast Rachel couldn't keep

track of them. His grandson also leaned close to watch. At last he lined the three in a row and peered up at her.

"Now choose, Mistress."

She pretended to study the thimbles, but when she reached out to the old man's mind she couldn't read him at all. Just her luck. As in her own time he was one of those people she couldn't read. Then she picked up the eager thoughts from another mind close by, and smiled.

"It's…'tis in the lad's right hand."

The little boy gaped at her, and then turned as if to run, but Evander caught him by the back of his tunic and lifted him off his feet.

"Tris, what are ye about?" the old man demanded before he gave Rachel a pleading look. "He didnae mean it, Mistress. 'Twas only mischief. He's a good lad."

"And a better thimblerig," Evander said and handed the boy over to his grandfather. "Give it over now."

Tris's bottom lip pushed out as he dropped the nugget onto the crate.

Rachel caught it before it bounced off and handed it to the grandfather.

"I'm sure he won't…willnae do that again."

"I'll be sure of it," the elderly man said and peered at her face. "Thank ye, Mistress, Master."

Once they walked away Evander said, "You saw the lad palm it?"

With all the villagers around them Rachel couldn't come clean about reading Tris's mind.

"I just guessed he had."

"I should have thought as much when the lad came to you," Evander said and nodded at the stalls ahead of them. "We'll have at the honest games now."

The next game Rachel tried was the sheaf toss, which required her to throw a heavy bundle of straw over rows of standing pitchforks. Her sheaf dropped a yard short, making her laugh. But when Evander took a turn with a much heavier man's sheaf, his cleared all the tines and thumped down beyond the last row.

"Ye throw like a spearman, no' a farmer," the big man running the game said as he gave Evander a small purse of coins. "Well done, Master Hunter."

At the next stall, an old woman ran something like a dice game. Seven small, carved stones were shaken in a cup before one was removed at random. Evander told her the stones were numbered from one to seven, and that to win she had to guess which one was in the old woman's hand.

"I will go see to the horses," he said. "'Twill no' take long. Stay here until I return."

"Sure," Rachel said smiling and joined the line waiting to play the game.

When her turn came she had every intention of guessing. Yet when the old woman felt the stone against her palm she thought of the number, and something made Rachel echo it.

"Seven."

"Aye," the old woman said. The thin hand opened to show the stone, marked with an X. "See ye the seventh as ken by the Viking, Mistress? 'Tis Gyfu, the rune of gifts, of love, of sacrifice. Will ye have a prize, or ken what I see for ye?"

Something about the old woman's eyes mesmerized Rachel. When she reached out to her mind, she saw a long tunnel, lined by trees that went on forever. The scent of the grove washed over her, cool and crisp, and for a moment it felt as if the sunlight had disappeared, and they were bathed in shadows and moonlight.

Evander came to stand beside her. "Have you won again, lass?"

Rachel felt the woman's thoughts suddenly cut off, as if a psychic door had slammed shut. Was she like her? Did she know that she'd looked into her thoughts? Or was it Evander?

"Ah, what do you see?" Rachel finally asked.

"Dinnae fear to speak of love, or to ask for mercy. Only ken ye must offer the same. Take it, so ye remember." She held the rune out to Rachel, but her cloudy eyes shifted to Evander's face. "'Twill need be squared by ye, lad."

Rachel tucked the rune in her skirt pocket as they walked away, and tried to joke about it.

"What do you think all that meant? No gift of love goes unsacrificed?"

"It meant she didnae have to give you a prize," he told her, sounding amused now. "'Tis an old Norse superstition, naught more."

"Well, at least I got a carved rock out of it." Another game where people were throwing iron circles at short wooden stakes in the ground caught her eye. "Hey, is that a ring toss?"

He followed the direction of her gaze. "'Tis called quoits. You must pitch the rings onto the spikes."

Rachel went over to watch the players, who kept missing or knocking over the spikes rather than ringing them. Once the players had all lost, the two women running the game hurried out to collect the rings.

That raven-haired wench has herself a fine-looking man, the younger of the two women thought as she eyed Evander. *Mayhap he'd like a lass with grander tits.*

Beka is pushing the pegs in too deep, her companion brooded as she surreptitiously tugged the wooden stakes higher. She glanced at Beka, and then continued loosening the pegs, unaware that she had skipped one. *Ogling the lads she'll never have, the stupit cow.*

Rachel picked up three rings and handed them to Evander, pointing to the stake that had been skipped.

"Do you think you can ring that one with all three?"

He gave the stake a measuring glance as he hefted the rings. "Aye."

Beka came over to collect Evander's money, and leaned over enough to display most of what her laced bodice could barely contain.

"Peg the three and you'll have your pick, Master."

Her coy tone made an icy heat bloom over Rachel's left breast, but before she could do anything Evander stepped between them. He tossed the three rings together with a jerk of his wrist, and they landed on the peg, circling it before they fell to the base.

Beka gaped, and everyone watching the game laughed or cheered.

"How did you do that?" Beka blurted out.

"My lady brings me luck," Evander said and surveyed the stand of prizes. He pointed to a small wreath made of intricately-woven ribbons and seashells. "That one she'll have."

Rachel didn't know what it was until he crowned her with it, and wove the trailing ribbons through her hair. She didn't smirk at the now-scowling Beka, but she did stand on her toes to give Evander a soft kiss.

"I feel like a fairy queen now."

"I saw the other one fixing the pegs to fall," he murmured as they walked on. "You chose the one she missed, but you couldnae have seen that. Her skirts were in the way."

"They were," she said and looked at the

people around them. She couldn't talk about it here. "I'll tell you later how I knew it."

"And what will you tell me? That you guessed it again, like the gold in the boy's hand, and the number on the old woman's rune?" Evander saw her expression and pulled her to a stop. "Rachel?"

"I heard her thoughts, and I saw what she was doing through her eyes. I read her mind, and the old woman's, and the boy's." She took his hand in hers. "I can read your mind, too. I've been doing it since I came here."

Evander guided her past the gaming stalls and tents and out into the glen, until they were well out of earshot of the fair-goers. Then he walked away from her, stood staring out at the sea for a few minutes, and came back. He looked at her as if she'd turned into a complete stranger.

"Since the night in the grove? Everything I've thought?"

Rachel nodded slowly. He had every right to be angry with her, but the thought of his temper exploding made her insides shrivel.

"Fack me," Evander said and dragged a hand through his hair. "Everything."

"I should have told you long before now," she said quickly, "but at first I didn't trust you. When I did, then I thought you wouldn't believe me, or it would ruin things between us. I tried to block your thoughts, too, but sometimes I couldn't help myself."

He studied her face. "Why no'?"

She took a cautious step toward him. "With you, I can do more than just read your mind. I can feel what you feel."

"And what do I feel now, lass?" he asked softly.

"Tense. You're trying to remember your thoughts since I came here." When he didn't say anything she plunged on. "In the beginning you felt annoyed, and impatient with me. You were still mourning Fiona, so you felt guilty for giving me her clothes and things. You were worried about how vulnerable I was, and you wanted to protect me. Most of all you really, really wanted to have sex with me." She saw his mouth curve and felt relief untying the knot of fear in her chest. "I knew I had to tell you, which I planned to do after we got home from the fair."

"I suspected you were some manner of seer," he said and tugged her up against him. "I never told you how to make morning brew strong, as I like it. That I needed the buckets for wash water when the rains came. How you ken where to touch me, where it most pleases me. Even that I wanted you this morning."

Rachel linked her hands behind his waist. "Oh, no. That last one isn't mind reading. You want me every morning." She peered up at him. "Why aren't you angry with me?"

"I should have guessed it. You're druid kind." He kissed her brow. "'Tis a powerful gift. You must be careful who learns of it."

"I was just worried about being around all these people. I thought I'd be smothered in all their internal voices. But so far in the crowd I seem to only catch a few stray thoughts." She glanced back at the stalls. "Except with that rune lady. I had a bit of a grove moment with her. I think she might be like me, too."

"Then we'll stay clear of her game," he said and hesitated for a moment. "If you've ken what I've been thinking, then I dinnae have to tell you what I am."

"An immortal Pritani warrior who's lived for twelve hundred years fighting with your clan against the undead. I didn't really believe it until this morning, when we were making love." Her eyes stung. "Then I saw everything."

"'Twas no' as bad as that," he chided gently.

"I've no' been a wise man, or a kind one, but I've fought worse. I didnae save Fiona. She saved me from my own dark heart. And now you, Rachel." He touched his mouth to hers. "I love you."

"Ho, Master Sheaf Tosser," a burly, grinning man shouted as he trotted toward them. "We've a spear throw setting up by the trees. Will ye test that great arm against us?"

Evander glanced down at her. "Shall I show the village lads how 'tis done?"

Rachel glimpsed a fragment of memory, when he had put down his spears by the shore of a serene lake. A moment later it was gone, but the sadness that came with it felt so intense she had to blink back tears.

Thank God he doesn't have to be alone anymore.

"I'd love to see that."

Chapter Eighteen

DIANA REINED IN her horse as Laird Gordon came out of his stronghold with a small entourage of guards to greet Lachlan and Kinley. Beside her Raen inspected the surrounding area before he dismounted and helped her down.

"We'll take them," she told the grooms who came out for the horses, and with Raen's help led the four mounts off to the huge barn. "Something is going on with Lady Gordon," she said, very casually. "Cap's all stressed out about it."

"The lady has a new bairn and a happy marriage," her husband said as he picked up a water bucket and emptied it into a trough so the horses could drink. "Why should our lady be upset?"

"Cailean's involved, apparently. Lady Gordon wants him to come over, and Druid Boy won't. Also, Laird Gordon has been doing a lot of riding around at night, remember? We've run into him at least four times on patrol this month." She removed the saddles and parked them on a drying beam before she rubbed the sweat from the horses' backs. "But it's no big deal."

"'Twas enough of a deal that she asked you to mention it to me." He eyed her as he hefted a sack of grain and went into the stalls to fill the feed buckets. "I dinnae ken anything about it, Wife. I dinnae think there is anything amiss."

"Uh-huh," Diana muttered. She led the horses one by one into their stalls, and then washed up before glancing out at the big house. "Cap thought I should have a word with the laird's bodyguard. Apparently he goes out with the laird every time he rides at night."

Raen pursed his lips. "It shouldnae be diffi-cult. Eamus is inside the house now with the laird." He grinned. "To be a bodyguard means one must guard the body, lass."

"Don't lass me, okay? I'm working on this." She dragged a hand through her hair as she looked around the stable. "Maybe we could lure him out here so I could cuff him to something. Only I don't have cuffs anymore, or a badge."

Her husband shook his head. "Wait here, and I'll bring him to you."

Diana frowned. "How are you going to do that?"

"Ask him to come." He avoided her swat and headed for the stronghold.

Five minutes later Raen returned with the laird's bodyguard, who was a good-looking behemoth of a man with an easy smile but watchful eyes.

"Great to meet you, Eamus," Diana said after the introductions were made. "We've been seeing the laird out riding at night when we're on patrol. Quite a bit, in fact. Are you having any problems around here we can help you with, maybe?"

His expression went from open to slammed-shut in a blink.

"No, Mistress Aber, no' at all. The laird has been having trouble sleeping, what with the new bairn in the house, and he rides at night to tire himself."

Diana knew a well-rehearsed speech when she heard one.

"Okay, that certainly makes sense. So where do you two ride on these insomnia-buster trips?"

The bodyguard looked puzzled. "Anywhere the laird wishes to go, Mistress. Generally out by the tenant farms, but sometimes in the woods. There's a small spring in the pines where my lord enjoys a bathe."

"Sounds like fun," she said, to which Eamus had no reaction at all. "Did the laird order you to lie to anyone who asks?"

"If he had, Mistress," the bodyguard said, "I wouldnae tell you. But no, I dinnae lie. 'Tis where he rides, and I am ever with him, as is my duty."

"Thank you, Eamus," Raen said before Diana could get in another word. "We'll no' keep you any longer."

The bodyguard nodded and headed out of the barn as if it were on fire.

"Why did you do that?" she asked as they watched Eamus pick up his pace to a flat run before he disappeared into the front gate.

Raen leaned against a post. "Do what now?"

"Man, he can really move for such a big guy." Diana turned on him. "Ah, you got him out of here so I wouldn't ask any more questions." She squinted at his impassive expression. "Oh, hell. You know about this, don't you?"

He held up his huge hands. "I was our laird's bodyguard for centuries. I ken only what 'tis to guard a man and his secrets, and be obliged to keep them both safe. 'Tis no' seemly to badger Eamus about what he cannae tell you."

"I don't badger," she told him, assuming a lofty expression. "I do, however, report to my boss, and Cap is not going to be very happy with you. At all."

"'Tis a banshee in a bannock," Raen said and reached out to take her hand and pull her close. "I ken naught of what Gordon does on his night rides, only that 'tis a closely-guarded secret."

"Well, you're no good to me," she said and slapped his chest. "I love that you're all about respecting the laird, but sometimes, Big Man, it's a real pain in my ass."

He dropped his hands down to caress that part of her anatomy. "When we're home, I'll kiss and make it better."

Chapter Nineteen

✿❀✿

E VANDER FOUND RACHEL the perfect spot to watch him on the far side of the spear throw field. Though most of the townspeople took the shorter walk to gather on the near side, a few of the women who had been cooking followed them to the farther side, where the view was unobstructed. Evander escorted Rachel nearly halfway to the targets and to the shade of silver birches.

"'Twill keep the sun from your eyes, the thoughts of the crowd at a distance, and the men from casting their looks at you." He pulled off his jacket and draped it around her. "Dinnae run off with all my coin."

She fluttered her eyelashes at him. "Win the prize purse, and I'll run off with you." As she sat down she felt the rune bounce in her skirt pocket, and took it out to hand it to him. "Here, for luck."

He bent down to kiss her before he tucked it in his pocket. "I dinnae need luck. I've you, love."

A dozen men walked out into the field with Evander, and chose spears from a tall wooden barrel. On the other end of the field, hay bales had been stacked in a row against the tree line. Over the front side of each bale a target made of painted cloth had been draped. Instead of the bullseyes Rachel expected, the villagers had painted crude figures of demonic-looking men with black eyes, white skin and pointed teeth. The targets looked exactly like the undead.

Rachel felt her skin crawl as she looked away from the targets and focused on Evander, who now held a long spear and stood at the throwing line.

The burly man marched up to the line and held up his hands until everyone quieted.

"One toss a man on the round," he called out. "I'll serve as judge for all three rounds. Head or chest are one point. Eyes or mouth are five. Ten points for the bastart's bawbag." He grinned as the crowd erupted with laughter. "If yer spears land outside, fall short or miss, ye're out. Ready to throw now, lads."

Evander and the other men hefted their spears, and eyed the targets.

"Away," the judge shouted.

Rachel held her breath as she watched Evander hurl his spear. He moved with such grace and speed it made her heart clench. His powerful skill became immediately evident when his spear outdistanced all the others in a blink. A few spears fell just short of the targets, while several others landed in the side of the bale or flew past it. Evander's spear hit his target with such force that it drove into the tree behind it.

The burly man walked out to inspect the targets. Six men were judged out, while most of the others were awarded one or five points. Evander's spear had skewered his figure in the groin, so he earned ten. Rachel cheered and clapped her hands as the burly man tied a white ribbon around Evander's upper arm.

Boys ran out to the targets to retrieve the spears and bring them back, while two men had to be summoned to remove Evander's spear. Rachel craned her neck to see if the tip was still intact.

"Here ye are, ye wicked hoor." A skinny arm clamped around her waist from behind, and a dirty hand stuffed a wad of cloth in her mouth. "Yer other lovers await ye."

Rachel screamed through the gag, and writhed as she tried to break free, but the man dragged her behind the birches and bound her hands and feet. As he did her eyes flared wide. He was Parnal, the drover she'd found lying to the shepherdess. He wrapped her in a heavy woolen blanket that covered her from head to toe, and then hoisted her onto his shoulder. His hateful, gleeful thoughts battered her like cudgels.

Can ye hear this, ye black-hearted cunt? I ken that you can. 'Twere my choice I'd take ye out in the woods and bind ye like a ewe for shearing. Then I'd beat ye proper before I'd fack ye in the arse. 'Tis how the evil one skewers ye, I reckon. I'd use ye as my pisspot, too.

As much as he wanted to violate her, Parnal wanted the coin promised to him more. He felt sure that the men he'd sold her to would do much worse to her.

Rachel tried to see where he was taking her, but hanging upside down with the edge of the blanket flapping over her face made it impossible. The sunlight grew thinner as he carried her into the woods, and followed a hard-packed dirt trail. As the last of the light faded he suddenly stopped and heaved her onto the ground.

The impact knocked the wind out of Rachel, and then Parnal yanked away the blanket and kicked her in the side as a group of men in heavy cloaks surrounded them.

"The facking witch herself, Marsters." The drover drew back his boot to slam it into her again, and squealed with rage as one of the men dragged him back from Rachel. "You should ken that she cursed me. I've no' a woman spread her thighs for me since she worked her foul magic on my poor soul."

A pale hand thrust a heavy pouch of coins into Parnal's hand.

"Say nothing of this to anyone," a cold voice said.

"Ye think me a fool?" the drover said. He shoved the coins in his coat, and crouched down. "Remember Parnal," he said to Rachel. "When they're gnawing and sucking on ye, Mistress, remember 'twere I who put ye in their hands."

He tried to spit in her face, but Rachel jerked her head aside before he could. One of the pale men seized him by the neck and shoved him away from her.

Rachel cringed as the pale men's thoughts slithered into her mind. They hungered to feast on her by sinking their sharp fangs into her soft skin and swallowing her hot, rich blood. Some imagined raping her over and over as they drained her to death, while the others fantasized about enthralling her and keeping her as a personal slave. All of their insidious desires remained in check by an order that kept echoing over their fantasies: *Bring the mortal female to the ship, but do not harm her in any manner. Any who disobey will be lashed to the punishment post and left to greet the sun.*

The only man who didn't have any thoughts of violating her was the same one who had paid off the drover. In his mind Rachel saw the sea, endless and eternal, and heard him think: *If the woman tells Quintus Seneca where he may find the highlander's castle, then we shall end the McDonnels and the curse. We can finally go home.*

That man stood over her as the rest of the pale men disappeared into the trees. They returned a short time later leading horses, one of which her guard mounted. Two of the others untied her and put her in front of her guard, who jerked the wad of cloth from her mouth. Rachel coughed and gagged.

"I am Optio Septus Lucanus," the man said. "I'm in charge of this detail. We are far from the fair, so screaming will bring no one to your aid, Rachel Ingram. Neither can you escape us." He pointed at the trees. "Try, and the boy dies a painful, ugly death, while you watch."

How had he found out her name?

Rachel turned to look as another pale man rode up the trail to join them, and almost screamed as she saw the limp little body of Tris, the thimblerigger's grandson, draped over his saddle.

"Do you understand me?" Lucanus demanded.

She swallowed bile and nodded, and the optio urged his horse into a fast trot, followed by the rest of the men. They rode out of the woods and down to the sea, where they headed west along the rocky shore. Rachel kept watching Tris, who thankfully didn't wake during the bumpy ride, and kept her back stiff to avoid touching Lucanus.

The short journey ended as they passed through three towering, eroded cliffs and entered a hidden cove, where several small oar boats had been dragged up onto the rocks. They launched the boats, and then carried her and Tris out to deposit them into the one manned by Lucanus and two of his men. One pulled the boy onto his lap and held a blade to his little neck as the other rowed with the guard. Rachel didn't see where they were taking them until the moon came out from behind the clouds and illuminated the silhouette of a huge black ship. That had to be their destination.

"I won't try to escape, or cause any trouble," Rachel said to Lucanus. "Please, take the boy back to his grandfather."

"No talking," he ordered and gave her a narrow glare before he regarded the unconscious child.

Rachel saw regret flicker over the optio's stern features, and opened her mind to his. At first all she felt was his cold, unwavering determination, but then a brief memory of a laughing young boy in the arms of a slender, pretty woman flashed through his thoughts. When Lucanus had sailed with the Ninth Legion for Britannia, he had left a wife and son back in Rome. While they had died long ago, he still remembered what it was to be a husband, a father, and to have something to protect.

They finally reached the black ship, where rope ladders were lowered over the side. Lucanus gestured for the other two undead to go up, and hoisted Tris over his shoulder.

"Please," Rachel whispered. "He's just a little boy. Let him go."

"I will ask my centurion if I may return him to his village." He gave Rachel a fierce glare. "But say nothing more of him, or the prefect will torment the boy to compel you. I have seen him do terrible things to children, Rachel Ingram. Now climb up."

She nodded quickly, and reached for the ladder. Her skirts made climbing up the slat rungs difficult, so she went slowly, and as soon as she was within reach of the crew they caught her arms and lifted her the rest of the way.

"Take them below," Lucanus said, and handed Tris to Rachel.

Rachel held the boy tightly as three undead guards marched her across the rough planks to an open hatch. There they took her down several short stretches of narrow steps until she entered a large hold that stank of sweat, vomit and urine, and had been filled with people in chains. Some were bruised, others had torn clothing, but all of them looked terrified. One guard pushed her down onto a low bench, and shackled her by the ankle to the ginger-haired, freckled woman next to her.

No one made a sound until the undead sentries left and bolted the door to the hold from the outside. Once they were gone, however, whispers, angry mutters and sobs filled the air. Two girls who looked like sisters hugged each other as they wept openly. A group of tonsured men bowed their heads and murmured prayers in Latin.

Even without reading their minds the fear and despair the captives felt saturated Rachel, who tried to clear her head by checking Tris. He had a small bump on his forehead, and a much larger one at the base of his skull, but his breathing seemed normal. She tried to gently wake him, until the freckled woman next to her touched her arm.

"Leave yer bairn sleep now," she said, and nodded at the door. "If he takes fright and cries too loud they'll come and beat him senseless. If that should happen, we'll gag him."

"My thanks for the warning, Mistress," Rachel said, taking care to use a Scottish accent. "He's no' my son. They took him from his grandfather at a village fair."

"Och, the poor wee lad. My name is Glenna." She brushed back a snarl of her light red hair and peered at Rachel's face. "Ye're no' a highland lass. Are ye come up from the south, then?"

She shook her head. "The west. I'm Rachel." She felt Tris shivering and held him closer to her, for the first time aware of how cold and damp the hold was. "Where are they taking us? Have they told you?"

"We go to our deaths, ye silly cow," a male voice said behind her.

"Hold yer tongue, ye arse boil," Glenna said. She scowled at him over her shoulder before she removed her shawl and tucked it around Tris. "There, that will warm him. We dinnae ken where we are to go. They clout us if we dare ask anything."

The hours crawled by as Rachel waited and watched the door. Glenna told her how she had been abducted while returning home late from the docks where she worked with her fishmonger husband. He had left early to make a delivery.

"I said to my Donald, if I walk alone in the dark they'll come for me, but did he listen? And now here I be." Glenna rubbed her arms. "At least he'll have to scale all his own fish now."

She half-listened to the other woman, but Rachel couldn't stop thinking about Evander, and what he would do when he found her missing from the fair. He had to know she wouldn't wander off on her own, and he was a superb hunter. He would do everything he could to find her, but if the ship sailed, so would all her hope that he would. She knew one thing: she'd rather die than tell the undead Tribune anything about Evander, his clan or Dun Aran.

This can't be the end of us, Rachel thought, her hands curling into tight fists. She had to do something to get off the ship and get back to her lover. Jumping off and swimming to shore wouldn't work. She'd freeze in the icy water or get dragged under by her skirts. Hiding somewhere might buy her some time, if she could get out of her shackles.

She reached down to feel the cuff around her ankle, which had been carved out of wood and had a metal loop. She was able to wriggle the pin holding it to the chain joining her shackles to

Glenna's, and tightened her arm around Tris as she used her free hand to push down on the top of her boot in hopes of prying her foot out.

The freckled woman nudged her. "Dinnae even think it, lass," she said in a low voice. "If they find ye've slipped from the chains, they'll take ye next."

"Take me where?" Rachel asked.

Everyone around them fell silent and still as wood scraped and the hold door swung open. Six undead guards entered, openly inspecting the faces of the cowering captives. The two young sisters were unchained and dragged from their benches, as were two other women and two of the monks. Then Lucanus strode in and came for Rachel.

As he unshackled her, she passed Tris to Glenna. "Look after him for me."

The other woman had paled so much her freckles looked almost black, but she clutched the boy against her breasts and nodded quickly.

Lucanus took hold of Rachel's arm as he brought her above deck, but there separated her from the other captives and hauled her to the bow. As the women behind her screamed and begged for their lives Rachel swung around, only to be jerked back to face the optio.

"My men must feed, Rachel Ingram, and you are too much temptation for them," he told her. "Stay here, and I will guard you until they finish."

She caught a glimpse of one sister being pinned to the deck by three snarling undead, who were ripping at her bodice.

"They're not just feeding, though, are they?" Rachel said. "Can't you control them?" She froze as the optio grabbed her jaw in a painful hold. "Oh, is that what you have planned for me, Optio? Or will your tribune do the honors?"

"Quintus Seneca does not want you for your lovely face, and I do not care to greet the sun." Lucanus let her go but leaned close to her, his eyes sheened with moonlight. "Tell the tribune what he wishes to know, and I will make you my thrall. You would be protected, Rachel Ingram. No other would use your body, or drink from your veins."

Again, she felt no lust from him, only a terrible, lonely emptiness that he hoped she might fill.

"I'm flattered, Optio," Rachel said as she probed his memories and misery. "But do you

444

think Darius would be proud of his father for enslaving and raping a woman? Would Petronia?"

His expression filled with icy fury, and he rammed her back against the inner hull and held her there by the throat.

"You dare speak of my wife and child to me? You are nothing but..." He stopped, and his expression shifted from outrage to confusion. "How could you know their names?"

"I know a great deal about you," Rachel said. "You were once a very decent man. A good husband, and a devoted father. You joined the legion so you could earn the money your family needed to buy land in the country." His hand fell away from her neck, but she kept going. "You were going to build a house there for Petronia, and teach Darius how to train horses."

Lucanus backed away several steps. "Do not speak of them, Rachel Ingram."

"Why not? They were your family. That's why you sent home most of your pay, and all of the spoils you shared in. Petronia was saving it for when you returned. You had a wonderful dream once, Optio." Rachel moved toward him. "But you've forgotten what it is to be human, and to have hope." She nodded at the women being stripped naked now. "They all belong to someone. Like Darius and Petronia were yours. Would you want that done to your wife? To your son?"

He looked as if he wanted to tear her face off with his teeth, and then his eyes lost their lethal glitter.

"I was a good man, a very long time ago."

He stared off toward the east, and then turned and strode over to where his men were preparing to rape the young sisters.

"Hold," Lucanus shouted. All the undead froze. "You have fed. That is enough. Take them below."

Chapter Twenty

DIANA WENT TO check on Kinley, who was visiting with Lady Gordon and her son, and then came downstairs to join Lachlan, Raen, and the McDonnel guards, who were meeting with Laird Gordon in his great hall. She still chafed over the fact that she had been unable to get a straight answer out of Eamus, or her husband, but the cop in her wouldn't stop until she had some answers.

In the hall Gordon's guards flanked two scruffy-looking men in chains, who smelled like old seaweed and stood with their shoulders hunched before Lachlan and Gordon. As she went to her husband, she caught their scandalized stares at the trews and tunic she wore, and smiled a little. She never tired of rattling the ever-chauvinistic mortal Scots.

"These two were just brought in," Raen murmured to her. "They've told a tale that no' even I can make out."

"Let me fathom this proper," the laird was saying to Gordon while eyeing the men. "You free traders claim that you saw a slaver ship attacking a merchant boat, boarding it, and then sailing off with nothing taken and no throats cut. Yet the merchant captain didnae report such an attack. No slaver has been seen on the north coast. We've only the word of you honest, trustworthy lads that it ever happened."

Raen cleared his throat. "Sampling that Flanders wine a bit too freely before bringing the bottles ashore to hide, mayhap?"

"Maybe," Diana said as she studied the smugglers' sweaty, fearful faces, and felt a tingle from her sixth serious trouble sense. "They look more like whiskey drinkers to me. Probably brought their own hooch along for the trip, my lord." She grinned at them. "Wonder why they're hauling untaxed wine. Isn't that illegal?"

"No' terribly, Mistress," Gordon said.

He glanced at the older smuggler, who was glaring at Diana.

"What is it, man?" Gordon said.

"The wench wears men's clothes," the smuggler muttered. "'Tisnae natural. Be she a witch?"

"Nope, sorry," Diana said and loomed over him. "I be a cop. That means if you give the lairds a hard time, I beat the snot out of you." She watched him cringe as she regarded his younger comrade, who looked more as if he wanted to share. She switched to good-cop mode. "All right. Tell us more about this slaver ship. What did it look like?"

"'Twas black as goose blood sausage, Mistress," he said eagerly. "'Twere painted with pitch, and fit with woad-dyed sails. Like a demon's boat was my notion, first time I spied her. No' one lantern light on her, neither."

Raen shook his shaggy dark head. "Raiders sail without lights, and pitching the lower hull avoids leaks."

"'Twasnae just that, Master," the younger smuggler said. "The slaver pitched her from stem to stern, and she had no portholes 'tall. Two day past she dropped anchor just outside our cove, barring our route, so we rowed out part way to have a better look at her. We couldnae see the cargo, for every inch of her were boarded over."

Lachlan froze. "The fack you say. Wood nailed over the portholes?"

"Aye, milord, and every other opening we could spy. I told Brenan 'tweren't right, keeping those wretched *traills* chained below decks with no light or fresh air." The younger man gave Gordon a keen look. "'Twas why we came straightaway to you, milord, without notion of any reward 'tall."

"This country has such upstanding criminals," Diana drawled as she glanced at her husband. "Undead using ships would explain why we've been seeing only small patrols on land. The rest of them could be scooting around on these light-tight boats."

"Do you mean they're no' slavers?" The younger man grew excited. "Are they the new raiders from the east, or the Sassenachs, bent on enslaving us?"

"We need to find this black ship," Diana told him. "Which direction did they sail from your cove?"

"Naught," the older smuggler said. "'Tis like I told ye, Mistress. They've been anchored there two day now." He scanned their faces. "The facking boat's still in our cove."

"Undead crews cannae sail by day," Raen murmured to Lachlan, who nodded. "But why would they wait?"

"They're not dropping off," Diana guessed. "They're picking up."

"That will be all, thank you," Gordon said and gestured to his guards, who swiftly removed the two smugglers. To Lachlan he said, "Ermindale had most of the northern slave trade before the king declared it unlawful. He had a goodly fleet of slavers to boot. The boat could be one of his."

Diana watched the laird walk over to a map on Gordon's wall, which showed the ports and harbors of the northern coast.

"After the battle at the marquess's estate," she said to Raen, "the clan found the bodies of Ermindale's entire family, murdered in the solar. But the laird wasn't among them."

"We assumed he was taken captive by the legion," her husband reminded her, and then lost his smile. "What is it?"

Diana held up one finger. "An old man like Ermindale wouldn't have lasted long as a two-legged blood bank." She raised another. "The legion is infantry and cavalry, not navy." She added a third finger. "The legion knew exactly which nobles to abduct in order to put pressure on the king's men, and yet they never tried to abduct them before they took over the marquess's estate."

His brows drew together. "You believe a noble like Ermindale helped the legion?"

"I think he was a vengeful, slave-trading jackass, so hell yeah," she admitted. "According to everyone he was pretty ancient, too. Just imagine if he offered Quintus Seneca a nice trade. Say, a whole bunch of slaves to turn into fresh troops, plus all those ships no one would suspect them of using, in exchange for immortality."

Raen touched his brow to hers. "You are a truly canny wench."

Diana went and repeated her theory to the lairds, and while at first Lachlan seemed skeptical, Gordon immediately seized on it.

"My wife and Ermindale's youngest daughter attended the same convent school," the young laird said. "Before she was killed she wrote Lady Gordon and said that her father had fallen ill with gut rot. He wouldnae have lived out the month."

Diana glanced at Gordon's bodyguard, who stood behind his laird and was watching the room. He was smirking, as if he were proud of his master, and then she knew why Raen had wanted to swear her to secrecy. But she had to put that thought aside.

"If we stake out the black ship tonight, my lord," Diana said. "I bet we'll find out why they've been attacking the merchants. With a little luck, we might even learn if the legion has a new stronghold."

"Somewhere only reachable by water, I'll wager," Gordon said. As they all looked at him he smiled thinly. "'Twould be what I'd do."

"You've a menacing mind behind that handsome face, lad," Lachlan said and stared at the map for a long moment. "Whatever comes of this, I'll no' let her sail again. Once we've learned why she's anchored, we take the ship before she can sail. We'll ferret out what we can from the crew, and then torch her."

Though Kinley decided to stay with the Gordons, Lachlan accompanied Diana and Raen as they left the stronghold. The laird took the lead and rode a short distance ahead of them.

Diana tugged on her husband's sleeve.

"Hey, we're going to take off any mortals we find on the ship before we set fire to it, right?"

"Aye, if any survive," Raen said. "They'll be imprisoned below decks with the undead. Once the legion wakes, they'll feed on them as fast as they can. Blood makes them stronger."

"Oh, no." Diana felt her stomach knot. "You mean–"

He nodded. "If we wake the legion before we can get below deck, they'll drain them dry."

Chapter Twenty-One

❧❀❧

THE JUDGE WALKED the line of targets with great dignity before he tromped back to stand in front of Evander and the other two men remaining in the contest.

"Five points to Geordie Larson for a right eye," he said and tied a yellow ribbon to the man's sleeve. "One point to Macken Trilby for a hit to the gut, which is of no great surprise to those who drink with him." He presented Macken with the red ribbon tied around a bottle of ale, which made the crowd laugh.

He then regarded Evander. "I've seen my share of spearmen, sir, when I served in the King's infantry. I've no doubt you're the finest ever to throw before these eyes." He tied the contest-winning blue ribbon to his sleeve. "Ten points to Master Hunter for a third straight cock skewering."

Evander had always been a proud warrior, aware of his finely-honed battle talents, but in this moment he felt more like the young mortal boy he had once been. In that distant time all he had ever cared for was practicing his throws out in the woods. He'd loved the simple beauty of the spear, and had kept at it until he could throw faster, longer and better than even the most experienced hunters of his tribe. That had been long before his Choosing Day, so only his youthful determination had driven him. The satisfaction of mastering the Pritani's most ancient weapon had made him feel strong and skilled.

Rachel made him feel the same. He'd once hoped he could be just a man with Rachel. Now, thanks to her love, he had become more. He had found himself again.

Sending the message while she had been playing the stones game had been a risk, especially now that Evander knew his lover could read his mind, but he couldn't take Rachel to the druids in the morning. He could never let her go now. Somehow he had to make peace with his clan, and find a way for the two of them to be together.

The crowd surged in around the three men, congratulating them with slaps to the back and shoulders, and squealing hugs from two proud wives. Evander looked over the heads of the villagers for Rachel, but saw no sign of her. His gaze shifted to the birches where he had left her, but only his jacket lay on the ground.

Mayhap she needed the privy, he thought, but remembered she had gone to the necessity just after they'd eaten.

Evander started wading out of the crowd, when the judge stepped into his path.

"Dinna go without your prize," the burly man said, presenting him with a bundle of finely-made hunting spears, and then frowning. "What ails ye, lad?"

"My wife has vanished," he said and quickly clasped the man's forearm. "I thank you for the spears, but I must find her now."

"Go with the gods," the judge said, and stepped out of his way.

Evander added the prize spears to his back harness, and sprinted across to the birches, where he picked up his jacket and looked all around them. Behind the trees he found a patch of bruised grasses and churned earth, and from there boot tracks leading into the forest.

He stopped at the tree line, where he found strands of long, black hair caught in some oak twigs. Rachel knew better than to walk strange woods alone, and the tracks from the birches were much larger than hers. As the sunlight faded Evander wheeled around, running for the pen of horses, where he retrieved his roan and paid the lads to stable the dappled gray overnight.

"To light yer way, Master," one of them said and held up a flaming torch for him. "Ye shouldnae ride out after dark. The blood-drinkers'll snatch ye up."

Mortals often gave such warnings, but Evander saw real fear in the lad's eyes.

"Have they been seen near the village?"

"Aye," the lad said and pointed toward the forest. "Last night, my sister saw one ride out from the trees to snatch a drover. He escaped later, but that doesnae mean ye will."

Evander had heard talk of the drover who had been chasing one of the shepherdesses. She grazed her flock close to Evander and Rachel's cottage. He tossed an extra coin to the boy.

"My thanks, lad."

The roan flew across the green and into the forest, where Evander reined it in as he held out the torch and looked for signs of recent passage. The disturbances he spotted in the brush and over the moss-carpeted forest floor led him to a bare patch of ground bearing the prints of several men and their horses. He dismounted and crouched on the ground where it appeared a small body had lain. He bent to sniff the soil, and smelled Rachel. He sifted through the dead leaves until he found a torn bit of ribbon and a broken seashell.

"So my nose doesnae deceive me. Ah, Rachel, love, I'm coming." He closed his hand over the bits and moved his torch to examine the boot prints, which showed a pattern of nail head marks he knew only too well. "Facking bastarts."

The men who had Rachel had been wearing *caligae*, the hobnailed marching boots of the Ninth Legion.

Evander mounted the roan, and made a circuit of the ground until he found the trail left by the undead's horses. That led him out of the forest and down to the shore, where the tracks disappeared into the rocks. If he went to the east he would only return to the village, and if that had been their intent the undead would never have taken Rachel away from it.

To the west he saw the shoreline curve away and disappear behind three columns of dark rock, shaped like giant spearheads thrust into the shore by the gods. Evander hissed in a breath as his ink burned across his chest. His war spirit came fully, flagrantly awake in him. But it didn't flood him with endless rage or prod him to gallop directly into a battle with the undead. It seemed to be tugging him toward the ground, so he swung off the roan and tethered it to a tree before starting down toward the sea columns.

Keeping to what shadows there were, Evander drew two of the prize hunting spears from his back and held them ready as he approached the rock soaring over his head. Beyond them he glimpsed an isolated cove where a dozen horses had been left to graze, but no sign of the undead or Rachel. He stepped between the towering columns and stopped, using the rock as cover as he inspected the entire cove, and noted the marks left by dories that had been dragged down to the sea. Stepping out from the rock, he peered out at the water, and saw the faint outlines of a black ship with no lights.

"Using boats, now, are you?" he muttered, moving closer to the water's edge.

It would take him only a moment to bond with the ocean and stream out to the ship, where he could board her with stealth and learn where they had imprisoned his lover. Then, once he got to her, he would—

"Well, now," a familiar voice said. A thin, sharp blade appeared under his nose, and dropped to press in beneath his chin. "How long has it been, Evander?"

Blood trickled down his throat as he jerked, the voice stunning him so much he couldn't speak until the blade dug deeper.

"But I killed you."

"Very nearly," Tharaen Aber said flatly. "Walk with me now, or you'll be talking around my dagger."

The laird's bodyguard yanked him back behind the sea columns, and marched him into a tidal cave. Inside stood Lachlan McDonnel and a large warband watching the ship.

"More dories coming, my lord," Fergus Uthar said, and pointed to a cluster approaching from the south. "Mayhap mortals."

The laird barely spared Evander a glance as he handed a torch to Neacal Uthar.

"I'll send the scouts to turn them back," Lachlan said. "Keep watch, and wait on Evander until I return."

Evander stood silently as a very tall, beautiful woman dressed like a man walked up to him and took Aber's blade to hold it while the bodyguard accepted some rope from a clansman.

"Hi there," the woman said, her accent sounding eerily like Rachel's. "I'm Diana Aber, Raen's wife. You must be Evander Talorc, the guy everyone wants dead. Including me, just in case you're thinking of making a move."

He saw a jagged mark on her palm that matched Aber's skinwork, confirming that she had been chosen as a mate by the bodyguard's spirit.

"Much has happened since I left Dun Aran," Evander said.

"Shut up," she said pleasantly. "Move a muscle, make a sound, or breathe hard on me, and I'm going to make the entire clan very happy." She tilted her head to one side to speak to Raen. "Really, I'm one of his tribe? I'm not seeing it. I mean, we're both tall, but he's got a jerk face.

Wait. Do I look like that, and you've just never told me?"

"No, love," her husband said, his tone a little softer now as he divested Evander of his weapons, and bound his wrists together tightly. "The hair."

Diana tugged back Evander's hood, peered at his head, and scowled. "All right, but mine's way, way prettier." She looked into his eyes, and tightened her grip on the dagger as she moved in another inch. "Oh, is that a move I see coming? Think I'm distracted, talking to my Big Man?"

He could see the Talorc in her eyes now. "No."

"Good," she said and bared her lovely white teeth. Then she leaned in, as if she meant to bite off his nose. "Because I'm not distracted. Not ever."

The threat she presented faded as Evander considered what her presence meant. Three women had crossed over from the future, all from San Diego. It couldn't be by chance.

"Where is Kinley Chandler?" he asked.

"That's Kinley McDonnel, the laird's wife to you," Diana said. "And it's no business of yours."

He wanted to ask them both if they knew Rachel, but shadows began filling the cave. The warband made way for a large group of druids lead by Cailean Lusk and Bhaltair Flen, who came to surround Raen, Diana and Evander. Beyond them Evander could see clansmen helping the magic folk drag their boats out of the water.

"Master Flen, Ovate Lusk," Raen said. He took the dagger from his wife, removed it from Evander's neck, and shoved him down on his knees. "Who summoned you here?"

"He did," Cailean said and nodded to Evander. "He sent a message by bird from a village fair not far from here. It took little effort for us to track him."

Bhaltair Flen came over Evander, his hair standing like a pale halo around his plump face.

"'Tis been a good while, Master Talorc. As soon as you broke your vow to deliver Mistress Ingram, we felt obliged to come and rescue her from you. Where is she?"

"The legion has her," he said and nodded toward the black ship. "On the boat."

"You delivered her to the undead?" the old druid exclaimed. He raised his arm, as his fist began to glow. "'Twill be the last of your betrayals."

"Turn off the nite-light, Grandpa," Diana

said and caught Bhaltair's arm and lowered it. "We can lower the boom later. We don't want the bad guys to find out we're here."

"The legion stole her from me at the fair," Evander told the old man. "I have been trying to protect—"

A huge boot filled his face, and kicked him over onto his side. Tormod Liefson appeared over him, his hands fisted and his expression rife with disgust.

"Seoc is gone. The shame you brought on him was so great he couldnae bear it. He gave himself to the legion in battle." The Norseman leaned over. "'Tis for the suffering you caused him that I'll end you, and I'll no' hurry it, you gutless worm."

Cailean surged forward. "Master Liefson, dinnae resort to violence."

"I wasnae always a map maker, Ovate," Tormod said. His pale eyes gleamed as he regarded Evander. "Nor have I forgot how we Vikings deal with betrayers."

Evander managed to raise himself back on his knees, and glanced around at the faces glowering at him. It made him sick to think of Seoc dead, but being held in such contempt by the clan gnawed just as deeply at his insides. For the first time Evander saw what he had lost when he'd run off with Fiona. Few of the McDonnels had cared much for him when he served as the laird's seneschal, but they had been his family. Dying might be the only way he could make amends, but before he faced the consequences he had to do what he could to save his lady.

"The lady from the grove is named Rachel Ingram," he told Bhaltair. "She is druid kind, with a powerful gift. I came here to take her back from the undead." He saw Lachlan walking into the cave, and shifted his gaze to Diana. "Release me and I will. Please, I beg you."

"Begging is good. We like begging." The tall woman crouched down in front of him. "Let's hear more about Rachel's ability. What exactly can she do?"

"She can hear thoughts, see memories and learn any secret hidden in the mind. She can read anyone." He braced his shoulders against the cave wall. "Since she became my mate she has seen everything in my head."

She recoiled. "You sick son of a bitch. You're *sleeping* with her?"

"She embraced the choice willingly." For once

he let his emotions show as he glanced down at Diana's fist. "I saw Aber's mark on your palm. You've mated, so you ken 'tis more than facking. 'Tis love."

"Yeah, I get it." Some of the lines around her mouth eased away. "Did they grab her because of her power, or to get to you?"

"I cannae tell you. They saw me take her from the grove, and somehow tracked us here." He lowered his voice. "If I may speak with the laird, Mistress Aber, I ken how to save her."

"Mistress Aber makes me think I'm cheating on myself with my husband. Call me Diana." She looked up at Raen, who nodded. "My lord," she called out. "You should hear what he has to say."

The McDonnels moved aside as Lachlan came and jerked Evander up onto his feet. In his dark eyes was as much hurt as anger.

"Tell me."

"I ken that my sentence is death. On my honor I offer you my life, willingly, if you will give me the chance to take Rachel from the black ship." He saw the laird's expression darken. "She doesnae ken you or the clan, nor any of you her, but we are mated. She loves me. When I am close, she will hear my thoughts. I'll tell her to jump overboard, into my arms."

Lachlan released him. "The lady trusts you this much?"

"Aye. Once I have her, 'twill take me only another moment to come to shore and bring her to you." When Lachlan didn't respond, he said, "If no' for me, then for the clan. She has the ability to see into any mind. I've no doubt she has all my knowledge of Dun Aran."

The laird's nostrils flared. "Neac. Come here."

The chieftain appeared beside him, and drew his double-headed axe.

"Permit me the pleasure of beheading this turncoat, my lord. 'Twould be a great favor."

One of the clansmen on watch rushed into the cave and came directly to Lachlan.

"My lord, we've sighted another black ship approaching."

Lachlan gestured for Raen. "Release him. Cailean, a word."

The bodyguard drew a dagger, hesitating as he eyed Evander's blood-streaked throat, and then stepped behind him and cut through the rope.

"We are no' finished," Raen murmured.

Evander nodded, and accompanied the laird, the chieftain and the druid out of the cave and down to the sea columns, where he saw the distant shape of the second black ship headed directly for the first.

"She's a brave lass, my lord," Evander said. "She'll no' tell them of Dun Aran."

"When they enthrall her," Neac said, "she'll lead them to our facking front gates." He then told him in terse terms about how the undead had discovered how to turn mortal victims into devoted slaves who would do anything, even kill, for them. "We dinnae ken how they do it, but the only manner in which to break their hold is to end the undead master. Unless we ken that we have, all mortal captives are considered undead allies. Like you, Talorc."

"I never helped the legion," Evander said as he dodged Neac's huge fist and stepped out of his reach. "I but took Fiona away. We lived along the highlands here, where no one could find us, until she—"

"Chieftain Uthar, please," Cailean said. As Neac came at Evander, the druid stepped between them. "Let the man have his say. 'Tis the last he will."

"Fiona died of pox. I buried her in the grove." Evander looked at Lachlan. "'Tis why this happened. I went there often to visit her grave. That night, I found Rachel clawing her way out of it. Somehow they changed places, but Rachel was still alive when she was put in the ground."

All three men exchanged long looks.

"We thought as much," the laird said. "Raen found your buckler."

He wished he could explain more, but he knew every moment he delayed Rachel could be suffering all manner of horrors.

"'Tis done," he said and nodded toward the anchored ship. "May I go to her?"

"No' alone," Lachlan said. "You'll take the druids' boat out to the ship. No one is to use water bonding. Cailean, we'll need you and yours to go first, and create a distraction so that Evander and the men may approach without notice and try his scheme. If it doesnae succeed, the warband is to board her and attack the crew."

Neac eyed the horizon. "'Twould be better to wait until dawn for a boarding strike."

"They'll no' be expecting the attack," the laird said. "Either or both ships may weigh anchor whenever they please and sail off in the dark. It must be now." He paused and glanced at each of them. "I want a moment alone with Evander."

Neac didn't look happy, and Cailean appeared faintly alarmed, but together they trudged back up to the cave.

"The ships are black because they've been painted with pitch," Lachlan said. "Likely they did it to keep from being sighted by the merchants they attack, and to seal the upper decks against sunlight. 'Twas a foolish mistake, but then they've never battled on the sea. They dinnae ken the reason why we Pritani never pitched our boats."

Evander eyed the anchored ship. "They've always fought on land."

"Aye," Lachlan said and took a tightly-sewn pouch from his belt, and handed it to him. "Do you recall what the Vikings did during the Siege of Paris?"

Evander checked the contents before tying it to his belt. "I'll see to it, my lord, as soon as I have my lady safe."

"You'll hand her off to Cailean, lad," the laird said. "For you'll no' be coming back with her. This is what you'll do."

Chapter Twenty-Two

R ACHEL WATCHED LUCANUS walk along the side of the ship like a caged feline, his thoughts becoming more savagely impatient by the minute. After stopping the rapes, he'd kept her with him, tying her hands together and shoving her to sit in a space between two water barrels. The stink of the dense black paint they'd used on everything gave her a low-grade headache, and she felt so thirsty she wanted to stick her head in one of the barrels.

A few undead crewmen remained on deck, but none of them paid any attention to her as they stood guard at various positions. Their thoughts only added to her general misery.

The optio is too soft on the captives. That guard

imagined beating the women until their bones fractured. *I would not be.*

Another relived past rapes while alternating with sullen repeats of *We always fuck the fresh ones when we feed.*

The cold night wind gradually dropped to an icy breeze, but the air grew so cold Rachel's arms and legs grew numb. She huddled in an attempt to preserve what body heat she had left, and nearly groaned when she saw tiny white flecks spiraling down on the ship's blackened planks. If it snowed too hard she'd freeze to death, which, given her current situation, wouldn't be as horrible a way to go.

Evander might not find her. She almost hoped he wouldn't now. He couldn't take on an entire ship of undead. A crackle of heat spread across her left breast, and she pressed her stiff hand over the spot to feel her ink moving over her skin.

Okay, she thought to her mating mark, *so maybe he can. It'll all be for nothing if I'm frozen to death.*

As if he could read her mind, Lucanus hurried over to yank her to her feet, and pointed to another black ship in the distance.

"The tribune has come, Rachel Ingram," he

said and caught her as her knees buckled. "What is the matter?"

She couldn't tell him she'd heard Evander say *I'm coming for you, my love* inside her mind, or that she'd deliberately fallen to make herself appear weaker than she was.

"It's so...so cold," she stammered. "I...I can't feel my feet."

"Since the curse we no longer grow hot or cold." The optio removed his cloak and wrapped it around her before he sat her down on a crate near the railings. He hesitated for a long moment before he untied her hands. "When the tribune comes, you must show respect. Answer his questions, and do not anger him. I think he will give you to me." He touched her shoulder. "I know you do not want this, but I am better than the others, Rachel Ingram. I will not feed on you. I will treat you as I did Petronia."

His desire for her poured into her mind again, but it had changed. Lucanus hadn't felt love since he'd been changed into a blood-drinker. When she'd reminded him of his wife he'd remembered his mortal life. He really believed that if he behaved the same way with Rachel that she would come to love him, as Petronia had. Now she had to lie and make him believe that she would.

"Thank you, Optio," Rachel said and forced her chapped lips into what she hoped was a convincing smile. "I'll do exactly as you say."

Lucanus crouched down in front of her, and drew her hands to his lips.

"We will be good together. I swear it."

Rachel read his desire for more of a show of feeling from her, so she took a deep breath, leaned forward and brushed her lips against his knuckles.

He dragged her forward until his mouth was only a breath from hers.

"Do you desire me, Rachel Ingram?"

The way he called her by her full name was starting to wear on her. So was his breath, which smelled like burned tinfoil.

"I hardly know you, Optio, but I would like the chance to be with you." She ducked her head to look modest, and so he wouldn't be tempted to kiss her. "To be honest, I haven't been with a man yet, so I'm a little shy."

Just as she guessed, the prospect of taking her non-existent virginity excited him even more. But his gush of fantasies about having sex with her made her stomach churn.

"I must see to the men now," Lucanus told her. "Stay here and wait for me, my lovely one."

As soon as he moved away and shouted orders for the sentries to prepare for the tribune's arrival, Rachel closed her eyes so she could listen for Evander again. She knew he couldn't hear her, but that didn't stop her.

Please, please hurry. The tribune is coming for me, and if you don't get here first I'm going to jump into the water and let myself sink to the bottom.

Rachel. Evander's voice seemed to resonate through her whole body. *I am waiting in the water. When the undead become diverted, you must jump off the port side, toward the bow. I will catch you, and my friends will take you back to shore.*

Rachel stared across the deck at the other side of the ship, and then glanced at Lucanus. Knowing Evander was so close made her want to hurl herself over the side immediately, but she'd never make it past the sentry standing guard.

"Halo to the ship," a mellow voice called out just beneath her.

Rachel leaned over to see two small boats, each being rowed by men in long, dark robes. One with a boyish face was standing and waving at the undead.

"We're sinking," the young man called up to Lucanus. "We willnae make it back to shore, and we cannae swim. Will you help us?"

Rachel waited as one by one the sentries came over to join Lucanus on the starboard side and fling down ropes to the robed men. When the way was finally clear, she lunged up from the crate and ran.

None of the undead grabbed her. Instead she slipped on the snowy deck and fell, skidding painfully across the slush-covered planks to stop short of the port side by a foot. Desperately she pushed herself up, and hurled herself at the rails, only to be seized from behind by hard, cold hands.

"This is your gratitude?" Lucanus said against her ear, his rage scalding her mind as his grip bruised her flesh. "You are a witch." He dragged her back from the side, and swung around to shout to the sentries, "*Defendi altus. Repulsus.*"

Rachel struggled against him as he hauled her back to the starboard, where she saw two empty boats floating beside the ship, and the looming shadow of something much larger. She looked over and shrieked as the second black ship passed within inches of her face, its wake hurling the two dories off on a huge roll of sea water.

Lucanus flung her over his shoulder, and started running, leaping over the rails and flying through the air. Rachel screamed as they landed, not in the water, but on the deck of the other ship, where they skidded into a pair of legs and she fell over onto her back.

Lucanus leapt to his feet and yanked Rachel to hers.

"Tribune," he barked. He jerked his head down and up, and shoved her forward. "This is Rachel Ingram."

The tribune looked down at her, his weathered face as inscrutable as his thoughts. The ruthless discipline of his mind felt to Rachel like a huge palace filled with tightly-locked iron doors and shuttered windows, with only his view of her appearing in the very center.

A pale blonde woman dressed in a modified legion uniform came from behind the tribune, and drew a dagger as she stood poised to attack. From her thoughts Rachel knew her to be a bodyguard, so focused on killing anyone who might harm the tribune that all she thought was of how she would strike the death blow.

"Report," Seneca said.

"The capture went as planned," Lucanus said, and detailed Rachel's abduction in brief. "I must warn you that this female is a brazen liar. Do not trust her for a moment."

"Brazen, is she?" An old man with the pale skin and the black eyes of the undead came to inspect her. "A mortal in need of taming."

"If you wish her to be tormented," the optio said, "I am happy to volunteer for the duty. This female tried to seduce me into becoming her protector. She even promised me her virginity."

"I doubt there's one part of her left that Talorc hasnae plumbed," the old man said, sounding bored now. "You should have her use her mouth on you. That's how I tell."

Rachel flinched as she looked away from Dougal, the Marquess of Ermindale. Behind his snide smile he had a mind like a cesspit seething with poisonous snakes.

Shouts came from the other ship, along with terrified cries and huge splashes.

"It seems the McDonnels have boarded the *Raven*, and are drowning the captives," Ermindale said, sounding amused. "Mayhap they think them witches, like this one."

"Optio, bring her below for questioning," Seneca said. "Do you wish to carry out the interrogation, Prefect?"

"I'll have Optio Lucanus attend to the wee hoor while I watch," the marquess said. "With that mighty leap he made, I wager he's earned the pleasure. And he wants her to suffer, so he'll be brutal."

Rachel cried out as the optio grabbed her by the hair, pulling at her scalp as he used it to drag her across the deck. As she twisted and kicked, the night sky seemed to explode, and burning rubble began to rain down around them. Pelted by embers, Lucanus dropped Rachel to strip off his smoldering tunic.

She staggered to her feet to see the masts of the other ship burning, and the undead crew jumping into the sea. Highlanders swarmed the decks, killing undead and tossing mortals down to dozens of men in dories. The stench of burning resin grew strong and acrid as the flames raced across the top deck, where a huge, jagged gap in the planks revealed the ruined deck below it. The highlanders jumped overboard, but one man remained behind, taking the wheel and turning it to bring the ship about.

"Set sail for the stronghold," Seneca ordered.

He began stomping on the little flames sprouting from the deck. Each time he did the flames divided and bounced away from his boot to burn in another spot.

"You cannae put it out, Roman," the marquess shouted, sounding furious now. "'Tis Pritani catch-fire. Naught can extinguish it but sand."

Rachel stared at the flaming ship now speeding toward them, her hand covering her mouth as she saw Evander at the wheel. He was steering the burning wreck directly into the path of the tribune's ship. He peered through the smoke at her, and took one hand from the wheel to touch the left side of his chest.

Undead rushed around her as more fires broke out, but all Rachel could feel was the gentle warmth of the mark he had given her, as if he were touching her through it. His thoughts were of her, and the days and nights they had shared, and how much she had given him. He knew, just as she did now, that no great design or immense purpose had brought them together. They had been two lost souls, battered and broken, abandoned and forgotten, and somehow they still found each other, and love.

Love was the reason.

Seneca and Ermindale suddenly flanked her. They took hold of her arms and rushed her over to the stern, where the tribune dropped over the side. Rachel landed in one of the empty dories, her body slamming into the hard wood bottom. The impact drove the boat down, and caused water to spill over the sides to soak her. The marquess jumped into the water with the tribune and several guards. They surfaced and crawled into the dory with Rachel.

"Take us to shore," Seneca ordered, but the rest of what he said became drowned out by an earth-shaking crash as the two burning ships collided.

Chapter Twenty-Three

❧❦❧

E VANDER LOST SIGHT of Rachel a few moments before the black ships smashed into each other. He looked back to see the mortals they had tossed overboard being seized by clansmen in the dories, who were rowing them back to shore. Evander could not join them. He knew the laird expected him to burn with the ships once he had used the pouch of catch-fire. For his crimes against the clan he would have let the fire take him, too, but he could not allow Rachel to share the same fate.

Pitch-fueled flames roared around Evander as he braced himself against the wheel for the collision. The burning main mast cracked, and with a loud splintering groan fell over onto the other boat. It crushed the undead caught beneath it. For a moment the smoke cleared, but Rachel had disappeared, along with the tribune and the old man who had been with her.

They willnae take her.

Evander felt his chest burn, and seized a spear dropped by one of the sentries before he took a running leap and jumped to the other ship. He landed and fell to his knees, righting himself onto his feet as a grim-faced Roman marched toward him, swords in both hands.

"Your slut tried to trick me, highlander," the undead shouted. "She will pay for it with her blood and her bones—"

He stopped and looked down at the spear Evander had buried in his chest, which clattered to the deck along with the pile of ash he became. Evander grabbed the spear as two snarling undead charged him, and he skewered one through the heart before he seized the other and flung him overboard. Swiveling around, he spotted the hatch to the hold, and shouted into it for Rachel.

A short sword jabbed at his face, but Evander spun out of the way, nearly thrusting his spear into the man's gut before he saw his condition and the bite marks on his neck.

"Ye shallnae harm me marster," the gaunt man hissed.

Evander knocked the sword from his shaking hand, and clubbed the mortal, who collapsed. Carrying him over to the side, he dropped him into one of the druids' boats, and saw the other being rowed to shore, with the Romans and Rachel inside it.

Dust blasted him, and Evander spun around to see Tormod drawing back his sword as if to strike another blow, with a pile of undead ash on the deck between them.

"To think you were once the clan's deadliest fighter," the Norseman complained as he jerked him away from the side. "I might have killed you just now. Me, the facking map maker. This wench has you entirely addled."

"Aye," Evander agreed and returned the favor by spearing another guard leaping down on Tormod from the crow's nest. "Yet your example helps me improve."

The Norseman peered down into the hold. "Enslaved mortals," he bellowed. "If you dinnae wish to burn along with these evil bastarts, drop your weapons and come up here."

Evander stood guard as Tormod helped the remaining thralls out of the hold. A few came with weapons, which he plucked from their hands before he hurled the thralls over the side into the sea.

"You see? If you're kind to the facking toadies, they bring you gifts." The Norseman gave Evander a short sword and another spear, and then took in the fire building around them. "We've ended their masters, so they'll no longer be enslaved. That's it, then. All that's left is you."

Evander waited for Tormod to attack, but something jerked him backward and he fell into the sea. Raen dragged him underwater as he swam across the cove and dragged him onto the shore.

"The facking undead wish to speak to you," the big man said, nodding at the undead between the stone columns. "Or they've promised to cut her throat."

Yanking off his soaked jacket, Evander saw the carved Gyfu rune Rachel had given him for luck tumble to the ground.

'Twill need be squared by ye, lad, the old woman had said. *Gyfu, the gift, the love, the sacrifice.*

Evander knew what he had to do now. He picked up his weapons.

Lachlan and Diana joined them, and flanked Evander as they walked toward their enemy.

"So the Viking didnae end you."

"'Twas a surprise to me as well," Evander said and glanced at the laird. "I expect he wishes more time to enjoy my suffering and screaming and such."

"We all do, honey," Diana assured him as they stopped a short distance from the columns. "This sucks. They've got perfect cover. Maybe if we put some men behind them."

"No time," Lachlan told her.

Rachel emerged from the shadows, the waves from the incoming tide crashing against the sea columns and soaking the bottom of her skirts. Quintus Seneca stood at her side, his stern face impassive as he regarded the McDonnels. Then Evander saw the dagger glittering against Rachel's throat, and behind her an elderly face appeared, wrinkled with a huge, fanged grin.

"So you survived the catch-fire, Talorc," Ermindale said. "You live up to your reputation as a slippery bastart. I quite admire you, you ken. Betraying your clan, running off with our spy, and remaining so well-hidden. And, of course, taking all of our new captives as well as this little witch. Did you enjoy her? Is she much skilled with her mouth?"

The old man was trying to provoke him into foolishness, which Evander ignored. He looked into Rachel's eyes, and knew she was sharing his thoughts.

"Release the lady, Ermindale, and I am yours."

"Oh, that's so not happening," Diana muttered.

"You think me a cunt to be stuffed with a cock of lies, then?" Ermindale tightened his grip on Rachel. "The moment she's free the McDonnels will kill you, and take her, and we'll have naught. No, traitor, I want the location of Dun Aran."

Lachlan made a disgusted sound. "He willnae tell you that, and even if he does, you'll never live to pay a visit."

Diana spread her hands. "There you go. Ask for something else."

"I think not," Quintus said softly.

The marquess looked past them. *"Parati."*

The mortals who had been rescued from the ship had quietly moved into positions behind the druids and the McDonnels. In an instant they produced daggers to press against the back of each clansman's neck, and every druid's throat.

"Son of a bitch," Diana breathed.

"For this," the laird said, his voice like ice now, "I shall gut you myself."

"Och, you'll permit us to do as we please," Ermindale said. "For I created each of these thralls. All I must do is utter another word, and they will slaughter the lot." He sent several soldiers up to collect horses before eyeing Evander. "Tell me the location now, or I slice your slut and end the rest."

"Have no doubt, he will do this," Quintus promised.

Diana shook her head. "If you tell him, my lord, he'll just do it anyway. He's that kind of asshole."

"We've no choice, lass," Lachlan said.

Evander hardly heard them as he held the gaze of the woman he loved.

I ken you hear me, just as you did on the ship. I cannae betray the clan to save you, but I willnae permit the undead to harm you. We've only one choice left. He showed her what he wanted to do to put an end to the stand-off. *I wouldnae ask this of you, but you willnae do it alone.*

The fear vanished from Rachel's face.

"I want what you want, Evander," she said. "Always. I love you."

"You are my heart," he said and tightened his grip on the spear as he nodded. "I'll be only a moment or two."

He lifted the weapon and threw it with all his strength.

Diana screamed as the spear buried itself in Rachel's chest, ramming through her heart. Evander knew he had killed her instantly, and felt as if his own heart were tearing itself in two. Behind Rachel the marquess stopped grinning, and uttered a strangled sound before his face turned gray and began to blow away with the wind. His arms crumbled away from Rachel's body, and a moment later his ashes dissolved into the sea.

The mortals holding the daggers on the McDonnels staggered away, now released from Ermindale's hold. Quintus Seneca stood over Rachel's body, his head bowed and his shoulders stiff. His female bodyguard rode up behind him, and pulled him onto her horse before she urged her mount into a fast gallop away from the shore. But Evander didn't pursue them. He rushed to Rachel's side and gently lifted her body from the water. As he slid the spear out of her and threw it away, he looked up to find Lachlan, Diana, and Raen.

"I would have chopped the old bastart to pieces," the laird said, gazing at the drifting ash. Then he turned a mournful look on Rachel. "Her end was quick."

"'Twas the only way we could save the clan and the magic folk," Evander said and stroked a hand over her dark hair. "She's always been a brave lass, my Rachel." He offered Raen the hilt of his short sword. When he didn't take it, he added, "You're owed this, and she's waiting on me. Aber, please."

The big man swallowed as he took the blade, and then dropped it. He shook his head and pulled Diana into his arms.

"Gods forgive me," the big man said, "but I cannae do it."

"You forget, Seneschal," Lachlan said. "'Tis my duty to reward bravery." He picked up the sword, and moved behind Evander. "Give your Rachel our thanks, Talorc. You go with mine."

Evander pressed his cheek to the top of her head, and smiled as the laird thrust down the point of the blade toward the back of his neck.

Always.

Chapter Twenty-Four

❧❦❧

MILLIONS OF STARS spangled the sky above the ancient tree canopy as Rachel walked to the center of the carved stones. Dying hadn't hurt a bit, thanks to Evander's strong arm and sharp eye. One moment she saw him throw the spear, the next she was back in the grove where it all began. That had a nice, full-circle feel to it. On some level she knew this place was more like a rest stop on the way to the next place, but that didn't bother her. As soon as Evander came they would go on together, as he had promised.

When she was with him she knew everything would be fine.

"Och, you're so sweet you make my teeth ache," said a light voice. A young girl walked out of the woods and came inside the circle. "Dinnae gawk at me like that. You remember me from the dreams. I'm Fiona Marphee."

"Yes, but you were a little older," Rachel said, appraising her, and then decided she liked her better as a teenager. "What are you doing here?"

"I've one more task before I can go on," she said, and sat down and patted the grass next to her. Rachel joined her. "'Twas brave, what you did. You saved the McDonnels and the druids, and you protected Dun Aran. You gave up your young life for them. 'Tis no small thing, lass."

"Yeah, and all I had to do was stand still. It was so hard." She wrinkled her nose. "It's strange, but actually it felt kind of wonderful to die that way."

"I cannae say the same of the plague," Fiona said and ran her hands over the smooth skin of her arms. "Do you ken that Evander never left my side, from the moment I fell sick to the night I died? He's wondrous loyal, that lad."

Rachel nodded. "So why are we here?"

"'Tis a good place, this grove. The oaks remember you, on this side and the other. They watched you grow from a wee lass, and they loved you." Her mouth flattened as she glanced at the grave they had shared. "They couldnae stop David, for you were needed here. 'Tis important to them that you ken this. They sent me to tell you."

Rachel glanced up at the lush green leaves shivering against the black branches, and felt a scattering of thoughts floating above their heads.

"They're not really oak trees, are they?"

"'Tis no' for us to fathom," Fiona said. She pulled up her knees and rested her chin on them. "The magic folk think they understand, but they dinnae. No mortal or immortal can. 'Tis the way of the gods." She gave Rachel a sideways glance. "He's coming now, so I'll get on with my work."

"Why can't you stay?" she asked as they stood up. "What do you have to do?"

"Weave the last threads of this cloth," Fiona said, and nodded toward a thin, smiling man waiting at the edge of the woods. "There's my da now. When 'tis finished, we'll go together to be with my mam."

Rachel's throat tightened. "Will I see my parents again?"

"Aye, someday," the girl said and smiled. "Give my love to Evander, lass."

Rachel hugged Fiona before she watched her

skip off to her father, who took her hand and vanished into the trees. The air around Rachel began to sparkle, and then the outline of a tall form drew itself before her, filling with color and light until it became the man she loved.

"Evander."

He caught her in his arms and held her, laughing as she rained kisses all over his handsome face.

"'Tis been only a few moments, lass. As I promised. We saved the lot of them, you and I."

"So we went out heroes." She touched his face. "Fiona was here, but for some reason she was much younger. She said to tell you…oh." The strange sensation in her chest made her look down to see her blouse turning to golden light. "What's this?"

"Your reward, lass." He bent his head to kiss her. "Remember that I'll be waiting. Always."

An unseen force jerked Rachel out of Evander's arms, and dragged her up into the twinkling night sky. Then she was falling into a sea of glowing hands, which caught her and showered her with light.

Rachel opened her eyes. The snowflakes clinging to her lashes blurred the faces looming over her. Her lungs filled with cold, salty air, and her arms shook as she pushed herself up from the grass. Smoke hazed the horizon, but the black ships were gone. She looked down and saw the tear in her bodice, and the blood soaking her clothes. The robed people around her drew back as she got up and swayed on her feet.

"What happened?" A confusing barrage of thoughts came at her from all sides, anxious and relieved, satisfied and awed. She saw a big man with a tattooed face wearing her lover's tartan, and asked him. "Where's Evander? Is he… Where is he?"

"It's okay, Miss Ingram." A tall redhead joined her, and glared at one of the older robed men. "You've had a bit of a shock. Why don't you sit down, and catch your breath? You've been through a lot today."

"I don't want to sit down."

Rachel pushed past her and turned around, looking for Evander but seeing only the faces of strangers. The men she passed ducked their heads, and then one who was almost as big as the tattoo-faced warrior came to her.

"Mistress Ingram, I am Lachlan McDonnel, laird of the McDonnel clan." He gestured toward the robed men and women. "These are your people, the druids. They can explain what has been done."

"I'm not interested," Rachel said just as she saw a tartan draped over a body down by the water. "Excuse me." She tried to get past Lachlan, and when he took hold of her arm she knew what he had done. She saw Evander's quick death, and the smile that had been on his face, and still it ripped through her. "You killed him? He saved you."

His dark eyes filled with regret. "Aye, lass, I did. 'Twas his last wish, to be with you."

"But I'm here. How can I be..." As understanding dawned, she backed away from him. "Oh, god. You let them bring me back, and heal me? How could you let this happen?"

"'Twas to reward you," Lachlan said sadly, "for your sacrifice."

"But I had that. We were together. That's all we wanted."

She turned blindly, and nearly bumped into Diana.

The tall redhead grimaced. "I know it seems awful, but it'll be okay, Rachel. You just need to take it easy now."

Rachel knocked her over as she ran as fast as she could to the covered body, beside which she fell on her knees. She drew back the tartan and gasped with pain as she looked down on Evander's still features. Her fingers shook as she brushed the hair back from his brow, and she bit her lip so hard she tasted blood.

The young druid came and knelt down on the other side of Evander's body.

"You must come away now, Mistress. There is naught more you can do for him."

She shook her head, and bent down to kiss Evander, the tears falling from her face to his. When she looked up she saw herself reflected in the druid's soft eyes, and saw past them into his thoughts. Evander's execution had appalled him, and he believed after her lover's heroic efforts to save the clan and the mortals that it was entirely unjust. Then Rachel looked deeper, and saw all the lives that Cailean Lusk had lived, and the terrible, beautiful magic that he and the others had used to bring her back from the dead.

Magic only druid kind could use. Druid kind like her.

"We can bring him back together," Rachel said,

as she curled her fingers around the back of Evander's neck, and grabbed Cailean's hand. "The resurrection magic is still inside him. Yes, I know it took all the druids to bring me back, but Evander is already immortal. The two of us can rework the spell inside him to heal the damage and awaken him again."

"How could you ken the spell is—" The druid went still, and the connection between their minds ended. "You cannae use me like this, Mistress. 'Tis no' my choice."

"He didn't deserve to die, and you know it," she told him flatly. "So you will help me do this or I'll tell the clan what I just saw in your head."

He took in a sharp breath. "You dinnae understand. 'Tis no' permitted for an ovate, or a novice to—"

"*Everything* I saw," Rachel assured him. Cailean glanced over his shoulder at where an older druid stood speaking with the laird, and Rachel followed his gaze. "And I'll start with them." Cailean's head whipped around and his eyes met hers. "I am deadly serious," she said, though her voice shook, "because I have nothing left to lose."

She watched him glance yet again at Lachlan

and then Evander. Finally, he gave her a tight nod.

"You are a reader," he said, "so you must join your thoughts to mine. Where I lead, you must follow."

She reached out to his mind so hard and fast that he recoiled.

"Sorry," she said quietly. "Go."

The druid's mind shifted from his worldly perceptions to a very different place. Rachel walked with him along a silvery path. It led into a forest of immense oak trees with emerald trunks and leaves made of amber light. The beauty seemed so immense and incomprehensible that she felt herself dwindling into something small and frightened.

You are beloved here, Sister, Cailean thought to her, and drew her into a grove where a perfect circle of carved stones surrounded Evander's body. *So it seems Evander is as well.*

Rachel refused to give into her fears. *What do we do now?*

I cannae wake him. The druid tucked his hands into his sleeves. *That is your task.*

She knelt down beside Evander, and clasped his cold hand between hers.

I know you can hear me. I know you're waiting. She tucked one hand under his neck, covering the wound. *I need you here, my love. Come back to me.*

Behind her Cailean murmured the words of the resurrection spell. Rachel felt magic pouring through her into her lover, and added all that she felt for him to it. The neck wound began to shrink beneath her palm. A moment later it faded away, and Rachel returned to her body. Her thoughts separated from Cailean's as the druid drew his hand from hers.

Evander's broad chest rose and fell, and his eyelashes parted as he peered up at Rachel.

"My lady, so soon." He lifted his head a little to look at the people walking down to them and let it drop again. "Fack me, no' again. Mayhap if they kill us together, at the same time, 'twill work proper."

"Let me do the talking this time, please," she said, and helped him to his feet as the laird approached them. "Good news, my lord. Laird. The gods have shown their mercy."

"Have they," Lachlan said, sounding unconvinced.

Rachel lowered her voice. "And not just to us. Imagine how useful it will be for the clan to have a mind reader." She glanced at Evander. "Not to mention the deadliest fighter in Scotland. And since Evander's death sentence has been carried out, there's no need to do that again." Her statement came out harsher than she'd intended, but Lachlan continued to listen. "I'm asking you to be the decent man I think you are." She gripped Evander's hand in both of hers. "Let him come home." She attempted a smile. "You'll never find a better Captain of the Guard or—"

"Enough of that," the laird said and rubbed his jaw. "Do you wish to return to the clan, Talorc?"

"I have all that I wish with Rachel, my lord." He wrapped his arm around her. "But I would be grateful for the chance to serve the McDonnel again, and I reckon the safest place for my lady is Dun Aran."

Lachlan appraised them both before he nodded. Then he turned to address the warband and the druids.

"The gods have shown their mercy," he said, though he gave Cailean a narrow look, "and returned Evander Talorc to us. For his sacrifice, and his courage, I pardon him of his offense."

"My lord, do you mean to welcome him back

in the clan?" Tormod demanded, and when the laird nodded, he regarded Evander. "Good." He saw how everyone stared at him and tossed up his hands. "Naught can kill the man. Even when you do, he comes back. Would you rather him an enemy?"

"No' me," Raen said and came forward, holding out his hand. When Evander took it, everyone cheered, so only Rachel and Evander heard him say, "Turn your coat again, and I'll give you to my wife."

Chapter Twenty-Five

S AN DIEGO, CALIFORNIA
Present Day

DAVID CARVER PACED around the interrogation room. Exhaustion dragged at him, but he hadn't been able to get a good night's sleep for more than a week. It perplexed him, for he'd always slept well, even after he'd murdered his wife. The nightmares had started just after his last trip to Vegas, and they were always the same: a dark-haired bitch in a robe chased him through a forest until he fell into a grave and the ground swallowed him up.

The weird thing was that the bitch wasn't Rachel, not with those gorgeous bazoombas.

David smirked a little. If Rachel had had that kind of rack, he might have let her live and just kept her too doped up to do diddly-squat.

The door suddenly opened, and a heavyset detective with curly gray hair stepped in.

"Who are you?" David demanded. "And why have you kept me waiting in here for an hour?"

"Detective Joseph Stuart with the Homicide Unit," the man said, but he didn't offer his hand. "I had to wait for some paperwork to be sent over from Financial Crimes. Sit down, Mr. Carver."

The words Homicide and Financial Crimes made him eye the thick file folder tucked under Stuart's meaty arm.

"I don't understand. Is this about Rachel? Was she in some kind of trouble?"

"Take a seat," the detective said and went around the table. He eased his bulk down onto the aluminum folding chair, and then looked up at David until he sat across from him. "Mr. Carver, you reported your wife missing on the morning after you were married." He opened the folder and skimmed the top page. "Monterey police responded to the scene, and found evidence that indicated she may have accidentally or deliber-ately drowned herself." He met David's gaze. "Do you want to add anything to the statement you made that day?"

He let his expression transition from outrage to suffering.

"I told them everything I knew. I also hired a recovery team to search the area for weeks, but they never found a trace of her."

"As opposed to looking for her yourself," Stuart noted as he drew a stapled document from the file and pushed it across the table. "This is a copy of a power of attorney that your wife signed just after you were married, giving you complete control of her estate. Is that your signature, sir?"

David pretended to study it. "Yes, it is."

"We interviewed the notary who witnessed your signatures, and the clerk who prepared your marriage license. Both women said your wife was pale, trembling and visibly disoriented." David gave the detective a bland look. "Was there a reason for her distress?"

"Rachel's parents died before they could see us get married. She was devastated by their loss, which is why we skipped the big wedding and had a civil ceremony." He blinked rapidly, as if to hold back tears, and then rubbed his eyes. He usually doused his fingertips with cologne to bring on real tears, but he hadn't remembered. "We were both very upset that morning."

"Is that why you purchased all these drugs, and this combat knife?" Stuart placed a stack of written prescriptions and a photo of the weapon in front of him. "In the event your wife got upset with you, so you could knock her out and solve your problems?"

"The sedatives are for me," David said blankly, staring at the photo of the knife. The knife he no longer had. The knife he'd left stuck in Rachel's back. God oh God, how could he have forgotten it? He hadn't worn gloves. His fingerprints and DNA were all over it. "Uh, I have trouble sleeping, so my doctor prescribed them. I bought the blade for personal protection."

"Really? I would never have pegged you as a knife fighter." The detective put a bank statement next to the photo. "Were you still upset when you cleaned out Rachel's personal accounts a week later? Did you need a sedative the week after that when you hired a very high-powered attorney to liquidate the remainder of her assets?" When David said nothing the detective gave him an easy smile. "It must be really tough to have a permanent suite reserved now at the biggest casino in

Sin City. How much have you gambled away since you paid off your bookies and that showgirl you knocked up? Five million? Ten? You do realize that accounts have to be settled here, David."

He realized the rapidly-hurled accusations hadn't mesmerized him as much as the photo of the knife. He'd have to go back for it. *Accounts have to be settled.* What did that mean, anyway? Now he didn't have to fake a shaky voice.

"I loved my wife, and I've been grieving ever since she killed herself. Look at me. I'm exhausted."

"Looks to me like you've been partying like there's no tomorrow," the detective said and took out a hand-written statement. "Your father believes that you murdered your wife for her money, especially in view of your recent behavior. He came to us yesterday, and provided us everything we needed to establish your motive."

David stared at his father's elegant hand writing, and recalled the vicious argument he'd had with Paul just after his last trip to Vegas.

"I see where this is going," he said. "My father introduced me to Rachel, did you know that? He wanted me to marry a rich woman. If he's trying to frame me so he can get at her money—"

Stuart's big belly shook as he chuckled. "Your father has an unshakeable, air-tight alibi. So does your mother, in case you're thinking of pinning it on her. They were both at the charity fundraiser for the entire day, and then had dinner with the governor that night." He cocked his head. "Was it an accident, Dave? You didn't mean to hurt her, but you argued, and your temper got the better of you? Did she find out about the gambling debts, or the showgirl?"

He doesn't have a body, so he needs a confession, David thought, and felt calm once more. He'd been too careful for the cops to prove anything.

"I'm sorry, but my wife committed suicide. Please don't call me Dave. I despise nicknames."

"Well, the party's over now, *David.*" Stuart gathered up the documents and returned them to the file. "Financial Crimes has obtained an emergency court order to freeze all of your wife's assets. By tonight I'll have the warrants we need to put everything you own under a forensic microscope."

Accounts have to be settled.

That reminded him: he should have put more

money overseas. But having all those lovely millions to play with had been impossible to resist. Now *accounts have to be settled.*

"We'll find her eventually, you know," the detective said. "When we do, you'll be moving into a permanent suite on Death Row."

"Are you going to charge me with anything?" When Stuart shook his head David stood and straightened his suit jacket. "If you need to speak to me again, please contact my attorney. Have a nice day, Detective."

David dropped his cell phone in a trash can on his way out of police headquarters, and drove his new Porsche around the city until he felt sure he wasn't being tailed. He then went to his condo, where he changed clothes and put on a fedora to cover his hair. Leaving the Porsche in the underground garage, he took his Mercedes on another roundabout drive through an industrial area before he finally felt secure enough to get on the highway and headed for Los Padres.

Checking his mirrors constantly, David deliberately drove past the exit for the park, and then doubled back. By the time he reached the oak grove, he had worked out a new plan. He would use his knowledge of his father's extramarital affairs to force Paul to recant his entire statement. He would even sue the San Diego Police Department for harassment, negligence and violation of his Fourth Amendment rights. He didn't intend to stay for the duration of the lawsuit, however. As a precaution he'd already transferred a million dollars to a Swiss bank. Once he bought a new identity, he'd fly to Monaco and restart his life.

All he had to do was get the knife he'd left stuck in his wife's spine.

David parked at the edge of the clearing, grinning as he climbed out. He'd have to brush up on his French so he could tell the women in Monte Carlo how he liked to have his dick sucked. The million he'd stashed away wouldn't be enough to keep him afloat, but maybe he could branch out, maybe do a little murder for hire.

The grass had grown over Rachel's grave, but he still remembered the exact spot. He'd never felt anything quite as thrilling as the moment he'd shoved the blade into her back. That was why he'd forgotten to retrieve the weapon. Before he left the US he might use it again on Paul, and cut out his tongue or slice off his balls. Maybe he'd make his mother watch.

After all, *accounts have to be settled*.

David took the shovel head and handle out of the duffle, and put the tool together before he began digging up the ground. Overhead the leaves made a rustling, whispery sound as he tossed aside shovelfuls of dirt and grass. When the edge of the shovel struck something hard he hooted with triumph.

"There you are, Rache."

He scraped away the soil from the decaying face, which now looked nothing like his dead wife. He expected her to smell rotten, but the scent rising from the earth was more like roses. He knelt down to push her body over to get at her back, and then noticed her clothes were wrong.

"What the…"

When he yanked at the full, heavy skirt she wore, it disintegrated in his fingers and fell onto the body in piles of rotted thread.

A skeletal hand latched onto his wrist, gripping it so tightly David felt his bones snap. A huge bolt of white-hot pain shot up through his arm, making him howl.

"Get off me!" he shrieked.

But when he fought the bony hand, it suddenly crumbled into dust, making him fall backward onto his ass. Before he could scramble to his feet roots began to shoot up from the ground and slither over and under him like tentacles.

"What the fuck is this?"

He grabbed the shovel and stabbed at the roots with the edge. Yet for every one he hacked through, two more punched up through the soil to wrap around him. The shovel fell from his hand as he became enveloped by the writhing roots, which seemed to be pushing him up off the ground.

The taste of dirt filled David's mouth as a root gagged him. The movements of the roots stopped for a moment, and then went in the opposite direction. His eyes bulged as the growths retracted outward, and he saw them wrapping around the oak trees. His limbs were stretched out in four different directions, and still the roots kept tightening and pulling on his body.

Tearing sounds filled the air as the seams of his clothes gave way, and then his joints began to pop. Pain ripped through him as he bellowed against the root crammed between his lips. His arms and legs dislocated and he knew it wouldn't stop. It would never stop. He was going to be pulled apart. This couldn't happen to him, not like this. He was a billionaire now. He was supposed to be living the good life.

The tugging of the roots slowed, drawing out the torture.

As agony blazed through his pelvis and torso David felt the root gagging him slide away, and he turned his head as something gushed from his mouth. He could see Rachel's grave, now filled with hundreds of white roses. The sweet smell of them filled his lungs, burning him from the inside out. Drops of blood fell onto them and streaked them red.

His body snapped as the roots pulled his right arm from his body, and then his left, and the last thing he saw was the ground rushing toward his face.

The oak trees stood sentinel as the roots dragged the pieces of David Carver's body deep into the ground. The shovel disappeared as well, while the roses in the grave grew pure white again, and then retreated into the soil as grass took their place. Above the hidden portal the veins of some oak leaves turned scarlet, but after a few moments the clearing appeared undisturbed.

All accounts had been settled.

Chapter Twenty-Six

❧❧❧

I SLE OF SKYE, Scotland
Fourteenth Century

HIGH IN THE ridges of the Black Cuillin, the
hidden stronghold of the McDonnel Clan seemed
filled with light and laughter, or so Cailean
thought as he escorted Rachel Ingram down from
her dressing room to the great hall. There the
entire McDonnel Clan had crowded within its
walls to witness the wedding ceremony of the lady
to Evander Talorc, their former seneschal whom
the laird had welcomed back and promoted to
Captain of the Castle Guard.

"Wow, there really are a lot of them," Rachel
said, sounding a little nervous. "I've been alone

with Evander in the mountains for all this time, so even the village fair seemed huge to me."

"All are good and kind men, but I expect you ken that. My master, Bhaltair Flen, sends his best wishes. He is in the lowlands attending to that wretched drover who betrayed you." Cailean stopped to accept a bouquet of white roses from a maid, which he placed in Rachel's hands. "A gift from your people."

She lifted the flowers to her nose and breathed in their sweet scent.

"But it's winter," she said. "Where in the world did you….oh." She smiled at him. "You enchanted some weeds. That's pretty incredible."

So was her ability to see into his mind. "The spell should last another day before they return to their natural state. I can teach it to you, if you like."

"You just did," she said and her expression turned rueful. "Cailean, I see that you're worried, but you should know that I've discovered something about my gift. I can only remember what Evander and I have shared." She glanced down at the flowers. "With the thoughts and memories from other people, after a day or so, they fade away. I'm a clean slate again."

The knot in his chest loosened. "So what you saw in my mind in the cove is gone now."

Rachel nodded. "Whatever secrets you shared are safe. Even the resurrection spell we used has disappeared from my memory."

Cailean knew the conclave had been considering more drastic measures to prevent Rachel from interfering in their plans, and felt glad that they would no longer be necessary.

"You have given me a great gift, my lady."

"Just remember," she warned, "I can always read you again."

Feeling very relieved, and somewhat disconcerted, Cailean escorted Rachel down the last staircase to the great hall. There he guided her up to the great hearth where Evander and Lachlan stood waiting with the visiting mortal lairds.

Cailean retreated to the upper hall to watch, and noted how Evander's harsh expression abruptly vanished the moment he saw his bride. The handsome smile lit up his face, and made the druid feel a rare surge of envy.

How would it be, to live forever with a love who would always be with you?

As for Rachel Ingram, now to be Mistress Talorc, Cailean would likely never feel especially comfortable around her. The ease with which she had plucked from his mind all he knew, including every detail of the Great Design, had staggered him. While it would serve no purpose for her to reveal it—and now he knew she had forgotten it —that knowledge was very dangerous indeed.

"She's a beauty," a low, sweet voice said from behind him, and Lady Gordon came to join him.

She wore a pale green silk gown that showed her delicate figure, now restored after her confinement, and a veil of golden lace over the smooth, heavy braids that crowned her head.

He remembered the nights they had shared when her hair hung down to her hips, and the touch of her hands on his slim body had driven him to take her again and again. What had been a sacred duty had become so much more that Cailean would always burn with guilt—and still he went stiff at the sight of her.

"I cannae help but agree," he said and glanced down to see Laird Gordon standing beside Lachlan. He liked the handsome young laird, who had always been congenial to him. He also hated him with every fiber of his being. "Shall I escort you to your husband, my lady?"

"That would be stupit, as he sent me to find

you." She stepped back and gestured toward the guest quarters. "Come, and I will show you why."

Cailean considered inventing an excuse to escape her, but none came to mind. Bethany Gordon's presence always reduced him to a callow boy.

"If you wish it," he said.

Lady Gordon led him directly to the bed chamber that she shared with her husband. Once inside she dismissed the maid watching over the infant in the bedside cradle. As soon as they were alone she lifted the plump boy into her arms and brought him to Cailean.

"We named him Danyel," she said and rocked her body from side to side as the boy's eyelids lifted. He made a low, cooing sound. "Will you hold him now?"

Cailean hardly heard her as he looked into the bairn's dreamy eyes. He had been chosen by the conclave to impregnate Lady Gordon because of his resemblance to her future husband, but the bairn was a tiny miniature of him.

"I dare not, my lady. I wouldnae wish to—" He gaped as she placed the little bundle in his hands. "My lady, what are you about?"

"I am introducing you to your son, Ovate

Lusk. Danyel, this is your sire." Lady Gordon folded her arms. "Dinnae make that face at me. Look at him. He is all over you. Do you no' see his eyes?"

"I cannae see the resemblance, my lady," Cailean said and took the boy over to the cradle and carefully placed him in it. "I am told that the difficult work of childbirth sometimes gives mothers strange notions." Dear gods, was this drivel actually spouting from his lips? "To my eyes young Master Gordon greatly resembles his sire, the laird."

"Surely he would, if Gordon had ever taken me," she said, tapping her foot now. "Which he hasnae, and willnae. To the world we may be husband and wife, but alone we are like brother and sister."

Cailean's jaw sagged. "Surely no'."

"Aye. When Gordon wishes pleasure he shares it with Eamus, his bodyguard. They grew up together as boys, and they've been lovers since they became men." Lady Gordon marched up to him. "Now tell me Danyel is no' yours, or that 'twas some miracle worked by the gods to bless me with a bairn. Isnae that what you were told to say?"

"Bairns often…'tis entirely likely that…oh, blind me." He dropped onto the edge of the bed and buried his flushed face in his hands. "Forgive me, Bethany. I never meant to do this to you."

She sat down beside him. "Cailean, 'tis no' as terrible as you think. When my courses stopped I knew to be honest with Gordon. Since we had no' been together, I didnae dare do otherwise. I told him that we had lain together before our marriage, and the bairn I carried was yours. I asked him if I might keep Danyel, and he agreed to raise him as his own."

He dared a glance at her, and saw tears sparkling in her soft eyes.

"But why should he," Cailean asked, "now that he has the truth of it?"

"The news thrilled him. He never expected to have a son, and he couldnae give one to me. We did try, you ken, for two clans depend on us, but with all women he is unable." She took out a kerchief and dried her eyes. "'Twas in return in part for my keeping secret his love for Eamus. You ken what would happen to them if they are ever discovered."

"I do," Cailean said and took hold of her hand. "If I had been aware of his penchants,

Beth, I would never have pressed for the marriage."

"Yet you would still have lain with me," she chided. "And found another husband to blame for siring Danyel, so the plan might continue."

Now she was scaring him. "I dinnae ken your meaning."

"Aye, you do. I've spoken with Lady McDonald, and Laird Darrow's betrothed. They both carry the bairns of druids who came to comfort them, as you did me. I expect there are many more." Before he could deny it she shook her head. "I dinnae wish to be told of whatever scheme you've planned. 'Tis no' why I asked you here."

Now she wanted something from him. He could see it in the stubborn set of her chin.

"Then why did you, my lady?"

"I've done what the druids wanted. Now 'tis my turn for scheming." Lady Gordon rose from the bed, and went to bolt the door. "Danyel will sleep for another hour, and the laird must attend the wedding feast. He will tell them that I am resting." She came to stand before him. "Take off your robe. I desire you naked for this."

He nearly fell off the bed. "We cannae. *Bethany.*"

"Och, Cailean, dinnae be such a dolt. You care for me, and I for you. Gordon understands, and approves. I'm determined that Danyel willnae be my only child." She dragged her bodice down until she revealed her milk-swollen breasts. "The druids need no' ken. 'Twill be our secret."

Cailean looked up at her, and saw the tenderness in her eyes as he began unfastening his robe.

"Aye," he whispered.

Chapter Twenty-Seven

❧❦❧

AFTER THE WEDDING ceremony, the feasting and drinking began. Rachel was hugged and welcomed by the clan as if she were a princess instead of the wife of their Captain of the Guard. She danced to the pipers with Evander first, who guided her through the gliding, circling steps of a reel. After that the laird claimed the honor of the second dance, which was a line dance consisting of spins and bows.

"No flings," Evander said as Neac approached her. "She's a wee little lass, and you'll break her."

The chieftain flapped a hand at him and led Rachel onto the floor, where he and the Uthars taught her their tribe's stomping, arm-flinging circle dance. By the time that finished she thought she would be flushed and out of breath, but it seemed that her new immortality came with endless vitality and excellent lung capacity.

"All right, boys," Kinley announced as she and Diana took Rachel's arms in theirs. "We ladies are going to get a little air and chat. Continue partying until we get back."

Rachel glanced at Evander as the women hauled her out through an arch and into the back courtyard.

"So what's this really about, my ladies?" she asked.

"She's the lady, I'm the cop," Diana said. "We've decided to form an all-girl mini-warband."

"Oh, yes," Kinley told her. "Because we are completely outnumbered."

While they were both acting a little drunk, Rachel sensed that was for the benefit of any men who might be watching.

"So how would that work?" Rachel said, smiling.

Diana laughed. "I'll track the undead, you'll pick their brains, and then Kinley will torch them."

"Great, I get barbecue duty again," Kinley

said. As they walked into the gardens, Lady McDonnel stopped and turned her vivid, white-laced blue eyes on Rachel. "Before all the killing and resurrecting, you didn't happen to find out if the legion has built a new stronghold somewhere, did you?"

"My reads fade away after a couple of days, so no," Rachel said, and explained the non-existent downside to her ability that she'd invented while talking to Cailean. Although she was lying through her teeth, both women looked as if they believed her. "I have a vague memory of something big near the water." At least that much was true. None of the undead had thought about their stronghold around her. She'd plucked that thought from one of the captives.

"Well, that rules out the lowlands," Diana said and dropped down on a bench. She took a swig from the wine bottle in her hand and passed it to Kinley before she shook out her skirt. "Since we're having our first unofficial chicks from the future club meeting, I vote we address a few things."

"This should be good," Kinley said to Rachel.

"The lack of comfortable clothing and the TP issue are my main bitches," the redhead declared.

"And then there are the fish and raisin punishment pies. Which have to stop, Cap, or Meg and I are going to rumble."

"The TP issue?" Rachel murmured to Kinley, and then realized what it was. "Oh, you know, birch bark works pretty well." When both women stared at her, she said, "Not the outside. The inside. It's really soft and absorbent."

Diana nodded. "So noted, plus points for creative use of nature."

"For clothing, we have tons of unused linen up at the cottage, too. Fiona couldn't go anywhere, poor girl, so pretty much all she did was weave." Rachel smiled sadly. "Would make great summer gowns."

"Now *I* want to marry you," the redhead said and sighed. But then she rose to her feet. "Oops, there's my guy, and he looks like he wants my gown off me. See you all when I regain consciousness and hobble downstairs, sometime tomorrow afternoon."

Kinley waved to Raen, and then asked Rachel to walk down to the loch with her.

"It's really been a lovely day, and I'm so glad you've joined the clan. We ladies are the minority, plus it's nice to have someone who doesn't need me to explain things like sports cars, basketball and cheeseburgers."

Rachel chuckled. "We should make some. We have almost all the raw materials here, except the ketchup."

"God, I miss tomatoes. Tomato sauce. Grilled cheese and tomato soup." The other woman sighed. "Okay, time for the serious stuff. My husband thinks you forced Cailean Lusk to bring Evander back from the dead. True or false?"

Rachel kept her expression blank. "What do you think?"

"I think you read his mind, and did it yourself, or made him help you. That's what I would have done." The laird's wife glanced back at the stronghold. "In a way it's good that your reads fade. But if there's ever anything you pick up that endangers the clan, tell my husband."

The cool detachment of her emotions surprised Rachel. "You don't trust the druids."

"I have my suspicions," Kinley said and grinned at her. "Go on, have a peek."

"Lady Gordon's son is the spitting image of Ovate Lusk. He might be one of your ancestors, as Gordon is an old family name." Rachel concentrated. "You're also pretty sure that Diana is Bhaltair Flen's direct descendent. Wow. That is interesting."

Kinley shrugged. "It could just be a wild coincidence that two of us came here, but I think you might have something to contribute to my conspiracy theory."

"My mother and father spent their honeymoon in Scotland," Rachel admitted. "For their first anniversary my father gave my mother a stone table she saw over there. That same table is sitting in Evander's cottage right now."

"Whoa," Kinley muttered and offered her the wine bottle. "Not to be extra nosy, but you look Italian to me. Where's the Scottish connection in your family tree?"

"My mother was Italian, but my father was half-Scottish. His mother's maiden name was Darrow." Rachel nodded toward the great hold. "In fact, I just met a Laird Darrow and his fiancée. I swear that lady has my dad's ears."

Kinley's mouth flattened. "Damn."

"I can read Cailean again, if you think it's necessary, but he'll be on his guard now," Rachel said. "People can hide their thoughts from me, like you did, when you brought me out her to talk about this."

"Let's hold off on that for now," Kinley said. She glanced past her and smiled. "Here's your husband, and mine."

Evander and the laird walked down to join them. After giving Rachel a paternal kiss on the cheek, and clasping forearms with her husband, Lachlan ushered his wife back to the stronghold. Rachel noticed Evander staring at one spot, and saw a flash in her own mind of the day he'd taken Fiona from the dungeon to run away with her.

"I didn't get a chance to tell you," Rachel said as she took his hand. "When I was in the grove with Fiona, she asked me to give you her love."

"'Tis how I shall remember her, with the same." He raised her hand to his lips. "Now, my lady, the laird has provided us with his lodge in the ridges for our wedding night. Lady Kinley has well-stocked it with a private feast and all we might want." He glanced up at the sky. "We may be snowed in for a day or two."

"It'll be like we're back at the cottage again. Just you and me, looking after each other, talking by the fire, and making love every night—but not just for a day or two." Rachel stood on her toes and pulled his smiling face down to hers. "That's going to be for the rest of our lives, my love."

THE END

• • • • •

Another Immortal Highlander awaits you in Tormod (Immortal Highlander Book 4).

For a sneak peek, turn the page.

Sneak Peek

Tormod (Immortal Highlander Book 4)

Excerpt

CHAPTER ONE

"Almost there, Gav," Jema McShane said, and squinted against the bleak mountain wind. She scanned the horizon before she helped her brother away from the car. "Isn't this a pretty spot?"

"Oh, aye, lovely," Gavin McShane said. He gripped the handles of his rolling walker and glanced at the surroundings. "It's Baltic out here, you mad quinie."

Twilight crept up from the horizon as the late

fall temperatures in the Scottish Highlands began a rapid plummet. In another hour they'd be courting hypothermia. Jema would have to be careful about how long she kept her brother out in the cold. Under his thick plaid woolens and trench coat, Gavin's joints and limbs had begun to resemble spindly kindling. His sluggish circulation made him chill easily. In his condition pneumonia was not only possible, it would be lethal. She'd misjudged how much time it would take to get him this far, but at least they were here.

Amyotrophic lateral sclerosis had been eating away at Gavin's brain and spinal cord for two years now. Because there was no cure for ALS, he wasn't expected to live far beyond three.

At least helping him along the dirt path from the makeshift parking lot to the Neolithic dig wasn't the ordeal she'd imagined. The grad students and volunteers working the site had carted out most of the heavy gear when they'd left for the day, packing the soil to a concrete hardness. Tomorrow they'd finish for the season by taking down the huts and collecting the cables and wires that provided power and lighting for the trenches.

How easy it was to ignore the fact that Gavin,

who two years back had been a healthy beast of a soldier three times her size, now barely weighed two stones more than she did.

"Reminds me of those tyre graveyards they have in Kuwait," Gavin said sounding bored. But at least he was looking around them. "Is this what they do with ours now?"

"Not typically. Usually they grind up tyres and pave the roads with them. All of Europe does."

She tugged gently on his arm to bring him to a halt on top of the plywood. Active excavation units were surrounded with the broad, thin boards, keeping the pit walls from collapsing by dispersing the weight of the excavators. Slowly, she and Gavin turned the walker around so the seat faced the site. As she set the brakes, he all but fell onto the padded cushion. But when he realized she'd been watching him, he sat up straight and took the torch from her. She gave his shoulder a gentle squeeze before she stood aside.

A foot in front of them lay the last open trench at the site, where she had been doggedly trying to find any sign of the burial she felt sure was there. Hundreds of old car and truck tyres surrounded it on three sides, stacked and waiting for tomorrow. In the morning, the pit would be backfilled with soil and draped with tarps, which the tyres would hold down and cushion against heavy snow drifts. Though the smell of the old rubber baking in the sun had made her sick over the summer, now it just made her feel sad.

But she still had tonight, Jema told herself as she took off her backpack, lowered it over the side, and let it drop. She pulled off her down jacket.

"Keep the torch light on me while I climb down," she said. "You'll be able to see where I've been working." She eyed the plywood under the walker. "Don't move any closer to the edge. The soil there is dodgy."

Gavin watched her tuck her jacket over his legs. "You're off your head, you know. What if you have a fall? I'm not leaping to your rescue."

"You can still use a phone, you great hell-beast," Jema reminded him as she extracted her mobile, checked the signal and then placed it in his lap. "Dial one-oh-one if I keep screaming, or nine-nine-nine if I stop."

"Maybe I'll call for a cab." He glowered at her, which made her feel like she was seeing her reflection in his face. He had the exact same gray-blue eyes she had. "Be careful, Jay."

Jema grinned and kissed him on the brow. Gavin hadn't called her by her twin name in ages. "Ever and always, Gee."

The short ladder extending down into the trench had been hand-painted with a V-9, designating it the ninth trench in which they'd found Viking-Age artifacts. The most exciting, an axhead still attached to a piece of wood handle, had been tentatively dated back to the first century BCE. Radiocarbon dating on the organics would be done back at the laboratory, but Jema wasn't interested in the weapon—it's what it might indicate.

V-9 was a burial pit. Jema would swear to it.

Of course they hadn't yet found a grave, or remains, or any indication a body had ever been buried here. Initially the trench had been filled with roots from several ancient, enormous oak tree stumps they'd found on the surface, which had made excavating it tricky. Jema had read several articles which speculated the Vikings deliberately planted trees over such graves in order to disguise and protect the dead, but she wasn't sure if she agreed. For one thing the tree stumps had been massive. When the tree ring dates came back, she wouldn't be surprised if they'd been planted a thousand years before the burial would have taken place.

The moment they had begun digging out the trench, however, Jema had begun feeling the oddest sensations. Her skin became acutely sensitive, while her heartbeat seemed to slow down. Whenever she touched a stone or root her fingers seemed to pulse with some frantic energy. She kept seeing in her mind the crude drawings she had studied depicting Freyja's Eye, even when she didn't want to think about them. She knew all of it was unprofessional, possibly delusional, and would get her thrown off the dig if she told anyone about it. So Jema had kept it to herself while she continued digging.

Now Jema reached the bottom of the trench and stepped off the ladder before waving and calling up to Gavin, "I'm in."

"You're daft," he called back, but kept the light from the torch trained on her. "There's nothing down there I can see. It's not but a big hole in the ground."

"That's because you're a soldier, not an archaeologist." Jema pointed to the feature she'd uncovered last week. "This is an inner wall face. The stones used to build it are these slab-like rocks called orthostats. They were stacked in parallel and vertical positions to create slots."

"Slots?" Gavin said and frowned down at her. "Like a casino?"

"No, like keyholes...or air holes." She took out a dental tool from her backpack and gently inserted the tip into one of the slots until it almost completely disappeared. "I feel something on the other side of this. It may be a created space, like a burial chamber."

He leaned forward to peer over the edge. "What, then, you want to unlock a grave?"

"Be careful," she said and eyed the position of his feet. "Don't put weight near the lip of the unit or the sidewall might give way." They'd already removed the stabilizing boards around the base of the pit. "You'll fall on top of my great discovery."

"A grave with slots," he mocked as he sat back.

"Or the final resting place of Freyja's Eye," Jema said and moved the probe to test another space. "Can you imagine it? A golden diamond the size of your fist, carved to honor the goddess's own beautiful eyes. Although it probably isn't even a diamond. It might be a fist-sized topaz, or a hunk of polished amber."

"Which can also use sunlight to melt off your

face," Gavin put in. "Don't forget that part. I've not, since you told me."

"That's just another myth," she assured him. "The Vikings always exaggerated their legends to strike fear in the hearts of their enemies. There's another one that says for every enemy that the Eye kills, it also takes the life of a loved one."

"So that's where they got that eye-for-an-eye thing," Gavin said and rubbed his brow. "I always thought that came from the Bible."

"No, it's actually from Hammurabi's Code," she told him. "Mesopotamian king of Babylon, and not a particularly forgiving man. You would have liked him."

Her brother made a rude sound. "Stop showing off how brilliant you are. Why are you so obsessed with this bloody rock? You can't sell it or keep it."

Her heart twisted as she shrugged and removed the probe. "The Eye will go to the National Trust, to be worshipped by countless generations of kids forced on museum outings. The find, however, would be mine. A discovery of that magnitude would get me a publication in every archaeological journal in the world. Edinburgh would finally offer me a full-time teaching position."

Gavin uttered a short laugh. "You hate Edinburgh."

She did, but that didn't matter. "I could take a flat for us near the uni, and get a home carer to look after you while I'm at work. You remember the doctor there who is testing that new drug treatment–"

"Jema, I'm going to die, and soon, and it won't be pleasant."

• • • • •

Buy *Tormod (Immortal Highlander Book 4)* Now

DO ME A FAVOR?

You can make a big difference.

Reviews are the most powerful tools I have when it comes to getting attention for my books. Much as I'd like it, I don't have the financial muscle of a New York publisher. I can't take out full page ads in the newspaper—not yet, anyway.

But I do have something much more powerful. It's something that those publishers would kill for: **a committed and loyal group of readers.**

Honest reviews of my books help bring them to the attention of other readers. If you've enjoyed this book I would so appreciate it if you could spend a few minutes leaving a review—any length you like.

Thank you so much!

MORE BOOKS BY HH

For a complete, up-to-date book list, visit
HazelHunter.com/books.

Get notifications of new releases and special
promotions by joining my newsletter!

Glossary

Here are some brief definitions to help you navigate the medieval world of the Immortal Highlanders.

Abyssinia - ancient Ethiopia
acolyte - novice druid in training
addled - confused
advenae - Roman citizen born of freed slave parents
afterlife - what happens after death
animus attentus - Latin for "listen closely"
apotheoses - highest points in the development of something
Aquilifer - standard bearer in a Roman legion
arse - ass

auld - old

Ave - Latin for "Hail"

aye - yes

bairn - child

banger - explosion

banshee in a bannock - making a mountain out of a molehill

barrow - wheelbarrow

bastart - bastard

bat - wooden paddle used to beat fabrics while laundering

battering ram - siege device used to force open barricaded entries and other fortifications

battle madness - Post Traumatic Stress Disorder

bawbag - scrotum

Belgia - Belgium

birlinn - medieval wooden boat propelled by sails and oars

blaeberry - European fruit that resembles the American blueberry

blind - cover device

blood kin - genetic relatives

bonny - beautiful

boon - gift or favor

brambles - blackberry bushes

bran'y - brandy

Brank's bridle mask - iron muzzle in an iron
framework that enclosed the head

Britannia - Latin for "Britain"

brownie - Scottish mythical benevolent spirit that
aids in household tasks but does not wish to
be seen

buckler - shield

Caledonia - ancient Scotland

caligae - type of hobnailed boots worn by the
Roman legion

cannae - can't

cannel - cinnamon

canny - shrewd, sharp

catch-fire - secret and highly combustible Pritani
compound that can only be extinguished by sand

Centurio - Latin for "Centurions"

century - Roman legion unit of 100 men

chatelaine - woman in charge of a large house

Chieftain - second highest-ranking position within
the clan; the head of a specific Pritani tribe

choil - unsharpened section of a knife just in front
of the guard

Choosing Day - Pritani manhood ritual during
which adolescent boys are tattooed and offer
themselves to empowering spirits

chow - food

cistern - underground reservoir for storing
rain water

claymore - two-edged broadsword

clout - strike

cohort - Roman legion tactical military unit of
approximately 500 men

cold pantry - underground cache or room for the
storage of foods to be kept cool

comely - attractive

conclave - druid ruling body

conclavist - member of the druid ruling body

contubernium - squad of eight men; the smallest
Roman legion formation

COP - Command Observation Post

cosh - to bash or strike

couldnae - couldn't

counter - in the game of draughts, a checker

courses - menstrual cycle

cow - derogatory term for woman

Coz - cousin

croft - small rented farm

cudgel - wooden club

da - dad

daft - crazy

dappled - animal with darker spots on its coat

defendi altus - Latin for "defend high"

detail - military group assignment

dinnae - don't

disincarnate - commit suicide

diviner - someone who uses magic or extra sensory perception to locate things

doesnae - doesn't

dories - small boats used for ship to shore transport

draughts - board game known as checkers in America

drawers - underpants

drivel - nonsense

drover - a person who moves herd animals over long distances

dung - feces

EDC - Every Day Carry, a type of knife

excavators - tunnel-diggers

fack - fuck

facking - fucking

faodail - lucky find

fash - feel upset or worried

fathom - understand

fere spectare - Latin for "about face"

ferret out - learn

festers - becomes infected

fetters - restraints

fibula - Roman brooch or pin for fastening clothes

filching - stealing

fisher - boat

fishmonger - person who sells fish for food

floor-duster - Pritani slang for druid

foam-mouth - rabies

Francia - France

Francian - French

free traders - smugglers

frenzy - mindless, savagely aggressive, mass-attack behavior caused by starving undead smelling fresh blood

fripperies - showy or unnecessary ornament

Germania - Germany

god-ridden - possessed

Great Design - secret druid master plan

greyling - species of freshwater fish in the salmon family

gut rot - cancer of the bowel

hasnae - hasn't

heid doon arse up - battle command: head down, ass up

Hetlandensis - oldest version of the modern name Shetland

Hispania - Roman name for the Iberian peninsula (modern day Portugal and Spain)

hold - below decks, the interior of a ship

holk - type of medieval ship used on rivers and close to coastlines as a barge

hoor - whore

huddy - stupid, idiotic

impetus - Latin for "attack"

incarnation - one of the many lifetimes of a druid

isnae - isn't

jeeked - extremely tired

Joe - GI Joe shortened, slang for American soldier

jotunn - Norse mythic giantess

justness - justice

kelpie - water spirit of Scottish folklore, typically taking the form of a horse, reputed to delight in the drowning of travelers

ken - know

kirtle - one piece garment worn over a smock

kuks - testicles

lad - boy

laird - lord

lapstrake - method of boat building where the hull planks overlap

larder - pantry

lass - girl

league - distance measure of approximately three
miles

Legio nota Hispania - Latin name for The Ninth
Legion

loggia - open-side room or house extension that is
partially exposed to the outdoors

magic folk - druids

mam - mom

mannish - having characteristics of a man

mantle - loose, cape-like cloak worn over garments

mayhap - maybe

milady - my lady

milord - my lord

missive - message

mormaer - regional or provincial ruler, second
only to the Scottish king

motte - steep-sided man-made mound of soil on
which a castle was built

mustnae - must not

naught - nothing

no' - not

Norrvegr - ancient Norway

Noto - Latin for "Attention"

Optia - rank created for female Roman Legion
recruit Fenella Ivar

Optio - second in command of a Roman legion century

orachs - slang term for chanterelle mushrooms

orcharders - slang for orchard farmers

ovate - Celtic priest or natural philosopher

palfrey - docile horse

paludamentum - cloak or cape worn fastened at one shoulder by Romans military commanders

parati - Latin for "ready"

parched - thirsty, dry

parlay - bargain

penchants - strong habits or preferences

perry - fermented pear juice

Pict - member of an ancient people inhabiting northern Scotland in Roman times

pillion - seated behind a rider

pipes - bagpipes

pisspot - chamber pot, toilet

plumbed - explored the depth of

poppet - doll

poppy juice - opium

pottage - a thick, stew-like soup of meat and vegetables

pox-ridden - infected with syphilis

praefectus - Latin for "prefect"

Prefect - senior magistrate or governor in the ancient Roman world

Pritani - Britons (one of the people of southern Britain before or during Roman times)

privy - toilet

quim - woman's genitals

quinie - a girl or unmarried woman

quoits - medieval game like modern ring toss

repulsus - Latin for "drive back"

rescue bird - search and rescue helicopter

roan - animal with mixed white and pigmented hairs

roo - to pluck loose wool from a sheep

rumble - fight

Sassenachs - Scottish term for English people

scunner - source of irritation or strong dislike

sea stack - column of eroded cliff or shore rock standing in the sea

Seid - Norse magic ritual

selkie - mythical creature that resembles a seal in the water but assumes human form on land

semat - undershirt

seneschal - steward or major-domo of a medieval great house

shouldnae - shouldn't

shroud - cloth used to wrap a corpse before burial

skelp - strike, slap, or smack

skin work - tattoos

smalls - men's underwear

SoCal - slang for southern California

solar - rooms in a medieval castle that served as the family's private living and sleeping quarters

spellfire - magically-created flame

spellmark - visible trace left behind by the use of magic

spew - vomit

spindle - wooden rod used in spinning

squared - made right

stad - Scots Gaelic for "halt"

staunch weed - yarrow

stupit - stupid

Svitiod - ancient Sweden

swain - young lover or suitor

swived - have sexual intercourse with

taobh - Scots Gaelic for "Flank"

tempest - storm

tester - canopy over a bed

the pox - smallpox

thickhead - dense person

thimblerig - shell game

thrawn - stubborn

'tis - it is

'tisnt - it isn't

toadies - lackeys

tonsure - shaved crown of the head

TP - toilet paper

traills - slaves

trencher - wooden platter for food

trews - trousers

trials - troubles

Tribune - Roman legionary officer

tuffet - low seat or footstool

'twas - it was

'twere - it was

'twill - it will

'twould - it would

Vesta - Roman goddess of the hearth

wand-waver - Pritani slang for druid

warband - group of warriors sent together on a specific mission

wasnae - wasn't

wee - small

wench - girl or young woman

wenching - womanizing or chasing women for the purposes of seduction

white plague - tuberculosis

whoreson - insult; the son of a prostitute

widdershins - in a direction contrary to the sun's
course, considered as unlucky; counterclockwise.
willnae - will not
woad - plant with leaves that produce blue dye
wouldnae - would not
ye - you
yer - your

Pronunciation Guide

A selection of the more challenging words in the Immortal Highlander series.

Bhaltair Flen - BAHL-ter Flen
Black Cuillin - COO-lin
Cailean Lusk - KAH-len Luhsk
Dun Aran - doon AIR-uhn
Evander Talorc - ee-VAN-der TAY-lork
faodail - FOOT-ill
Fiona Marphee - fee-O-nah MAR-fee
Lachlan McDonnel - LOCK-lin mik-DAH-nuhl
Loch Sìorraidh - Lock SEEO-rih
Neacal Uthar - NIK-ul OO-thar
Seoc Talorc - SHOK TAY-lork
Tharaen Aber - theh-RAIN AY-burr
Tormod Liefson - TORE-mod LEEF-sun

Dedication

For Mr. H.

Copyright

Making Magic

✣

Welcome to Making Magic, a little section at the end of the book where I can give readers a glimpse at what I do. It's not edited and my launch team doesn't read it because it's kind of a last minute thing. Therefore typos will surely follow.

Story is character. Period. Full stop. So why pick a traitor from the first book in the series to feature as my new hero? Because we all begin as something else.

Even in the first book, it was clear to me that Evander had backstory. A character like him doesn't just jump onto the page fully formed. A forceful and opinionated personality is forged in the past. Be it mostly genetics or mostly environment, we're all shaped by where we came from.

That seemed doubly true for Evander, and I knew I had to dig in and find out how and why.

You've just finished reading the book so I won't get into the details, but the bird's-eye view is this: I want to believe that we're all capable of change. If Evander and Rachel can manage it, I think there's hope for us too. :) And if love is the great motivator, so much the better.

I know some readers were nervous after seeing the title of this book when it was put on pre-order. But I hope I've allayed your worries and that you enjoyed seeing these two people transform. I'm pretty glad to see them join our clan of immortal couples after really earning their place in that growing family. I hope you're glad too!

Thank you for reading, thank you for reviewing, and I'll see you between the covers soon.

XOXO,

Hazel

Los Angeles, October 2017

When will it cool down??

Read Me

Like Me

Grab My Next Book?